SUMMER READING
IS KILLING ME

AMY E. LILLY

Library of Congress Control Number: 2015906379

1st Edition

©2015 Amy Lilly
Bella Lilly Press
Spanishburg, WV

Cover Art by Ashley Townsend.

ISBN-13: 978-0-692-434253

DEDICATION

FOR DENNIS.

CHAPTER ONE

I love summer and how the air ripples as waves of heat rise from the asphalt. The warm summer breezes sway the large trees surrounding the lake. I love the buzz of the bees as they zip from flower to flower. One of the best things about summer is cruising down the road in my 1968 VW bus, Velma with the windows down, the wind tangling my strawberry curls and my favorite music playing on the radio. My summer love died when I discovered a dead body in Longfellow Park. Too bad I left my Super Librarian costume hanging in the closet that day.

Just after dawn, I was unloading tables for the Miller's Cove Founder's Day Celebration. The town library holds an annual book sale during the festivities to raise money for the children's party at the end of summer reading. I planned to meet Wade, my library clerk and general dogsbody, at eight to unpack the books. Unable to sleep, I decided to set up tables and hang our banner by myself before picking up Wade. Clint was at the state police headquarters in Burlington for the next few days for training, and I was keeping his Jack Russell Terrier, Watson. I was busy hauling things to our designated spot when I heard frantic barking. I spotted Watson growling at something in the grass under the large oak tree.

"Watson! Come here, boy!" I whistled. He looked up but kept barking. With a sigh, I jogged over to shush him before he woke up the whole neighborhood. As I came nearer, I stopped. A young woman was asleep and oblivious to the little dog nipping at her feet. I bent to wake her and saw a splash of rust red across her shirt and a silver-handled paintbrush buried in her chest. Scattered on the ground next to her was a canvas, an easel and some tubes of paint with bright colors oozing out the open ends.

"Oh crud!" I said aloud. Watson lunged forward with a snarl and tugged at the bottom of the woman's jeans. "No, Watson! Come here!" I picked him up and carried his wriggling body to Velma. I pulled my cell phone out of my bag and called the sheriff.

"Miller's Cove Sheriff's Department. What's your emergency?" A nasal voice answered. It was Tina, the gum-smacking, fingernail-polishing receptionist who aspired to be a cop one day as long as the uniform didn't make her thighs appear fat.

"Tina, it's Ophelia Jefferson. I'm over at Longfellow Park and I found a girl dead. Someone murdered her."

"What? A dead body? Murdered? Are you sure?"

"Yes, I'm sure!" I snapped. "Can you send a deputy right away?" I shouldn't be surprised Tina doubted me. There hadn't been a murder in Miller's Cove in over one hundred years. It all changed when my friend Grant's mom, Shari Davis, lost her grip on reality and murdered three people last year. If Clint hadn't charged in and rescued me, I would have been next. A scar above my left eyebrow served as a reminder of my ordeal. It gave me a slightly impish quality with a hint of danger. A James Bond meets Jane Austen flair.

"Mark's on duty this morning. I guarantee he's over at Nellie Jo's having a cup of coffee and a doughnut. I'll call and send him right over," Tina said.

"I'm not going anywhere," I said and disconnected. I heaved a sigh and loaded the tables back into Velma. My gut feeling was the Founder's Day Celebration would be canceled.

CHAPTER TWO

Deputy Mark Thompson pulled up in his cruiser ten minutes later. I'd known him my whole life. He retired from our small sheriff's department a few years ago but discovered retirement bored him silly. His wife, Sally, didn't want him underfoot driving her crazy, so he went back to work part-time which made everyone happy. A sleepy town most the year, the crime spiked when people rented cabins by the lake for the summer. Most calls involved overturned and damaged trash cans from the local wildlife with an occasional domestic dispute thrown into the mix.

"Morning, Phee. Guess you found yourself a body. Tina says you think it's a crime scene." Mark took a sip from the Nellie Jo's Joe-to-Go cup in his hand. I would kill for a cup of coffee right now. Some people ate comfort food. I drank comfort caffeine.

"She's underneath that large oak tree." I pointed. "Mark, somebody stabbed her in the chest with a paintbrush. It's awful." I shuddered in spite of the morning's warmth. I led Mark over to the body.

"Did you touch anything?" Mark asked. He squatted next to the girl. His eyes combed the ground looking for evidence.

"No, I didn't." I shook my head. "Watson found her and tugged on her pants leg. I got close enough to grab him, but I was careful."

4

"You recognize her?" Mark stood up and walked around the body, his brown eyes cataloging the canvas and paint on the ground.

I examined her face. If it weren't for the ghastly gray pallor of death, she would have been beautiful. It was a face someone would remember. "No, I've never seen her. There's a women's art retreat at the lake this year. She might be one of the artists."

"I need to cordon off the area and call Sheriff Dawes. He won't be happy. I wouldn't want to be in his boots when he tells Mayor James to cancel today's event," Mark said. "Do me a favor, Phee. Stay by the body while I go back to the cruiser to get crime scene tape and my kit. This area should be secured before folks show up for Founder's Day and trample any evidence."

"I'll guard it with my life," I promised. Mark loped across the grass to his vehicle. Who stabbed somebody with a paintbrush? An angry art critic? I inspected the body and noticed one finger covered with blue paint. I walked around and looked closer at the canvas lying on the damp grass. The painting was an unfinished landscape with a large slash of blue the same shade as the paint on her finger. I moved closer. Was that a letter? I couldn't tell because of the smearing of the paint, but it resembled a cross. Was this a message from the victim? I pulled my phone out of my pants and snapped a few photos of the painting before Mark returned.

CHAPTER THREE

Sheriff Dawes arrived and took charge of the situation. The mayor pulled up a few minutes later. Mayor James declared the celebration cancelled until further notice. I left after Mark took my statement and headed to my parent's to drop Watson off for his play date with their dog, Hamlet. I told them about finding the body and reassured them repeatedly that I would be careful. I promised to see them the next morning for breakfast and to retrieve Watson.

Word spread like wildfire through town that the mayor canceled the Founder's Day Celebration due to the discovery of a dead body in the park. As I drove back into town and passed the park, I slowed to a halt due to the first traffic jam ever seen in Miller's Cove. People gawked as EMTs removed the body to transport it by ambulance to the coroner's office in Burlington. By the time I made it to Nellie Jo's for a cup of coffee, the place buzzed with speculation on the victim's identity and who murdered her.

"I overheard it was some la dee da gal from the cabins on the lake," Nellie Jo gossiped as I ordered my coffee and scone. Nellie's deep Southern drawl hadn't faded despite all her years living in Miller's Cove. "Why, I bet you anything it was some kind of love triangle. Rich folks always cheat on each other. They cheat on their taxes, too."

"I didn't recognize her as anyone from around here," I confided. I leaned across the counter and lowered my voice, "She was young and pretty with long, blonde hair."

"You saw her?" Nellie's eyes widened. She handed me my coffee and blueberry scone.

"I was setting up tables for our book sale when I found her," I told Nellie in a conspiratorial whisper. "She was under the giant oak tree with all the initials carved in it."

"Golly day! I'm just glad you didn't run into the killer down there! You've been through enough after last year with that Davis woman. Speaking of which…" Nellie pointed her chin. I turned and saw Grant Davis walk in the door. I made a point of avoiding him since his mom tried to kill me. He had stopped by the hospital after the attack, but my family refused to let him in to see me. Since then, we stayed away from each other. I couldn't dodge him here in the small café though.

"I can tell him he's not welcome," Nellie offered. She stepped out from behind the counter to intercept Grant.

I felt torn between letting Nellie protect me and confronting the situation with Grant. "No, it's okay. I can handle it." I sighed and carried my cup and plate over to a small table by the window. Grant had lost both his parents - one to death and one to insanity. He had his own demons to contend with, and I felt a momentary twinge of sympathy for him.

"Phee, can I talk to you?" Grant stood in front of me. His handsome face was gaunt and his clothes hung on his already slim frame. His mother's crimes and subsequent committal to a mental institution had taken its toll on him. It wasn't his fault his mother killed three people, but the sight of him brought the horror of the day with

Shari rushing back. I felt sick to my stomach and shoved the scone across the table.

"Ummm… I guess." I refused to meet his eyes. I stared at my cup as I struggled to control my emotions. My hands shook as I lifted my coffee to take a sip. The coffee shop had buzzed with gossip when I arrived, but now it was strangely quiet. Nellie Jo wiped the clean table next to me and tried to appear uninterested.

"Phee, I'm sorry. I miss your friendship. Please tell me how to fix things between us," Grant pleaded. He reached out to touch my shoulder, but I flinched. He dropped his hand and sighed.

"Grant, we're friends, but right now I can't separate you from your mom. Why can't you comprehend that? I can't see you without reliving that horrible day. I almost died!" I stared blindly ahead blinking away tears.

"I understand. I wish I could turn back the clock. I spotted you in here and had the crazy idea to ask you to watch the early movie tonight at the theater. We can sit next to each other, share Jujubes and slushies, and try to remember what it feels like to be best friends again," Grant said. "We don't have to talk and you can't see my face in the dark. It was stupid. I'm sorry I bothered you." He turned to leave.

I sorted through my emotions. Grant was the same guy he'd always been. He was still the guy who picked me up in his old Dodge Dart and wasted our teenage afternoons cruising with the windows down and the music blaring. "Okay. I'll go."

Grant stopped and turned around to make sure he hadn't misunderstood. "Pick you up at six? Jujubes and slushies are on me." A hint of the old Grant emerged.

"Sounds good. See you then," I said. Grant gave me a smile and left.

As soon as the door closed behind him, Nellie rushed up to my table and laid a reassuring hand on my shoulder. "Are you okay, Phee? You look mighty piqued. You should've let me kick him out of here."

"I'm fine, Nellie. It's just hard seeing him. Now we've got another murder in Miller's Cove, and once again, I'm in the thick of it. Juliet says bad luck comes in threes, so I've certainly met my quota," I said. I lifted my cup to my lips and took a sip. "If it weren't for your good coffee and scones, I'd be a nervous wreck." I patted Nellie's hand to reassure her that I was okay.

"You mark my words. This latest murder was about love and money. When a pretty, rich girl gets murdered, a man is probably involved and money is at the heart of it," Nellie predicted.

CHAPTER FOUR

I bought two coffees to go and headed to the library. I had called Wade when I left the park to tell him about the canceled celebration. He wanted to hear about the crime, but some things should be shared in person. I walked in and saw Juliet sitting on the circulation desk.

"Have you lost your ever lovin' mind?" I exclaimed. Juliet jumped down and gave me a guilty look. "Wade has clearly lost his mind letting you sit your derriere on the desk. Good golly, Juls, were you raised in a barn?"

"As a matter of fact..." Juliet gave me a cheeky grin. "Sorry, Phee. Nobody was in here. Everybody's milling around by the park to see what the police learned about the murder."

"Either there or at Nellie Jo's grabbing a cup of coffee with a side of gossip," Wade said as I handed him the cup I bought for him.

"I didn't realize you were here or I would have brought you one, Juliet," I apologized.

"That's okay. I'm here to find out the real deal about what happened in the park. That and to check out the hot guy behind the desk pushing subversive books on the innocent townsfolk of Miller's Cove. He tried to make me read *The Scarlet Letter*. The nerve! So what's the skinny, Minnie, with the murder?" Juliet leaned forward and fixed me with her best detective interrogation glare. After our pitiful attempt at crime detection last year almost got me killed, Juliet immersed herself in the world of crime – fact and fiction. She read as many mystery novels as she could and watched cheesy, 1970s cop shows during her free time. I had created a monster. A yoga-loving, granola-eating, Nancy Drew wannabe monster.

"What makes you think I know anything?" I grabbed the *Miller's Cove Courier* and pretended to read the headlines. "I see they are planning to build a new subdivision down by the lake. It's called Shady Retreat."

"Aargh! Spill it!" Juliet screeched as she snatched the paper out of my hands.

"I'm guessing it was one of the summer renters here for the artist's retreat. She was young, blonde and pretty," I lowered my voice and glanced around to make sure the library was empty, "Don't breathe a word, but somebody stabbed her in the chest with a paintbrush."

"Jiminy Christmas! That's a horrible way to kill someone!" Juliet exclaimed. She clapped her hand over her mouth when she realized how loud she was.

"Shush! No one is supposed to know that little detail," I admonished her. I briefly considered showing them the pictures I took on my phone, but decided to hold off for now.

"The cops kept a piece of evidence back from the press so they can identify the perp. Smart." Juliet narrowed her eyes. She tried for wise cop but came across more like a crazed Pomeranian.

"You've been watching way too many police shows from the seventies," Wade chuckled. "I can't imagine Clint saying perp when he discusses a case with Sheriff Dawes, but I could be wrong. For all I know, they might sit around with their feet on the desk and eat doughnuts all day."

"I've been wracking my brain to figure out how you kill somebody with a paintbrush. Wouldn't the handle break?" I recalled the crime scene and the wound in the girl's chest. Something about it seemed odd. Like someone staged it.

"Wait a minute. Paintbrush?" Wade made a motion like he was painting the side of a barn.

"An artist's paintbrush, silly, not a paintbrush for painting walls. That would be too bizarre. There was an unfinished canvas and easel on the ground next to her. I guess we'll wait until they release more details about the crime to find out who she was and who killed her," I said.

"We should investigate and solve the crime ourselves. Clint's out of town. The sheriff is short-staffed since the new deputy isn't here yet. We could help," Juliet said. Wade and I both turned and gave her open-mouthed stares. "What? Don't stare at me like I've gone bat guano crazy. We found clues last time. Phee used to be the only one with investigator knowledge. Now that I've read every Agatha Christie novel in the library, I'll be a real asset. Besides," Juliet rummaged in her purse and pulled something out, "I made us both the coolest crime fighting accessory ever."

I shook my head as I saw what Julie pulled out of her purse. She held two hot pink masks she had obviously sewn herself. A bedazzled 'L' was on the forehead of one and a 'Y' on the other. "Okay, 'L' I get. Super Librarian. But, Juls, I'm dying to know. What the heck does the 'Y' stand for?"

"Super Yogi!" She exclaimed.

"Lord love a duck, but I believe you've gone mad," I laughed.

CHAPTER FIVE

"The two of you scare me sometimes, and this is coming from a guy who's been to war." Wade shook his head as he watched Juliet and I try on our masks. I had to admit that I liked my hot pink mask much better than my boring black one I made last year. "I don't have enough in savings to bail you both out of jail if you get caught doing something crazy. Do I rescue my girlfriend or the lady who signs my paycheck? Decisions. Decisions."

Juliet leaned over and gave Wade a quick peck on the lips. "No worries. Now that I'm in the game, there is no way we can get in trouble. Besides, the masks are for fun. I doubt we'll ever be lucky enough to wear them."

"Listen up, Super Yogi, our first task is to identify the victim. She wasn't a local, so we should go to the rental cabins by the lake and snoop there first," I suggested. I felt safe nosing around a stranger's death. No ties to me meant no danger.

"You want to go down there this evening?" Juliet asked.

"Sorry, I can't. I forgot to tell you. I ran into Grant at the coffee shop. We're going to a movie tonight."

"Have *you* lost your ever lovin' mind?" Juliet parroted. "Oh, wait. I don't even need to ask because I know you have. There is no way you'd catch me hanging out with him again!"

"It's hard to explain," I hesitated while I formed the words to explain my decision to still be friends with Grant. "It's not Grant's fault his mom is crazy. He's been my friend for so long I need to at least make an effort to keep the friendship going. Grant's a good guy. To be honest, I looked at him today, and it was like seeing a kicked puppy."

"You're a better person than I am. I'd leave that kicked puppy at the pound. I need to go adjust my chakras and try harder to forgive," Juliet said. "What's Clint's opinion of this movie date?"

"It's not a date. It's two friends figuring things out after a shared trauma," I protested. "And Clint doesn't know because he's in class all day today. I'll call him tonight before I go."

"Whoa. Good luck with that one." Wade gave a low whistle. "If it was me, I'd be pissed if Juliet went to the movies with a man whose mom tried to kill her. Clint must be more evolved than I am. Me, Tarzan. You, Jane." Wade beat his chest. He grabbed Juliet around her waist and pretended to swing on a vine. She giggled and kissed Wade. They were good for each other. Wade brought Juliet down from the clouds, and she made Wade take life a little less seriously.

"Clint doesn't have a jealous bone in his body. He knows how much I pine for him every day and long for his sweet kisses at night," I simpered in my best bodice-ripping heroine voice. I batted my eyelashes at Wade and clasped my hands to my heart. "I just can't live without my big, strong lawman."

"I just threw up a little in my mouth," Juliet gagged. "Be serious. Once we know who she is, we can find out who hated her enough to kill her. I'll mosey down to the park and see what I can overhear." Juliet grabbed her bag off the desk and started towards the door. She paused and looked over her shoulder. "I'll talk to you later, my big hunka chunka burning love." She blew Wade a kiss and sashayed out the door.

"Hunka chunka burning love? Hmmm...I need to change the name on your personnel file." His face turned bright pink, and he busied himself by straightening the newspaper to put back on the rack.

"She just said that to tease you. Behind closed doors, I'm her Sugar Booger," Wade deadpanned as he headed over to the reading area to shelve new books.

"I think I'm the one that just threw up a little. We'd better get busy unloading all the boxes of books still in my van. We'll have to see if they reschedule the Founder's Day Celebration or cancel it altogether. In the meantime, I need to supervise Juliet's detective work before she gets herself into a pickle." I snapped my fingers at a sudden thought. I reached over and picked up the phone to ferret out my first clue. "I know the perfect person to help me figure out who that girl was."

CHAPTER SIX

"Stone Street Gallery. Nicolette Simonton speaking."

"Nic, it's Phee Jefferson over at the library," I said. Nic and I knew each other from volunteering with the kids at the Miller Cove's Parks and Recreation Department Summer Camp. I did story hour and crafts with the younger children while Nic taught beginning art to the tweens and teens. "I wanted to ask you a quick question."

"Phee! It's good to hear from you. What's up?"

"I had the misfortune of discovering a murder this morning down at the park. You might have heard about it through the rumor mill."

"It was all anyone could talk about when I grabbed my cup of coffee today."

"I hoped that you might know who the victim was," I said.

"Me?" Nic sounded surprised. "I don't see how in the world I can help."

"She was in her early twenties with long blond hair. Very attractive. She was painting a landscape. She could be here for the artist's retreat."

"Petite with long blonde hair past her shoulders? Sounds like Elody Campbell. She brought me a few pieces to sell in the gallery. I was thrilled to take her art on commission because she has talent. Her paintings are amazing."

"Do you know anything about her? Was she attending the artist's retreat?"

"Aren't these questions for the police to ask? I don't mean to sound rude, but aren't you sticking your nose into something that isn't your business?" Nic's voice tightened.

"You're right," I said. "I'll pass Elody's name on to the police. I was curious about who she was since I found the body. I appreciate your help." Nic wouldn't understand my urge to investigate the murder myself. She probably thought my interest was a little ghoulish.

"Not a problem. I wish I could tell you more, Phee, but go ahead and pass Elody's information to the sheriff. I'll be happy to help them however I can. Take care of yourself." Nic disconnected the phone. Perhaps I just imagined it, but her voice seemed to have lost its earlier warmth.

I felt bad for upsetting Nic, but then gave myself a small mental kick. The one thing I learned from my near-death experience last year was that I wasn't responsible for everyone else's feelings. I picked the phone back up and dialed the number for the sheriff's office.

When Tina answered, I asked to speak to Mark. "You haven't found another body, have you? I swear Miller's Cove is turning into a veritable hotbed of crime."

"What? No, I wanted to tell Mark the victim's name is Elody Campbell."

"Thanks, but we've already identified the victim." Tina lowered her voice, "Mark's down at the lake. Turns out somebody broke into one of the cabins and turned it upside down. He's trying to investigate the break-in and the murder. Sheriff Dawes is on damage control calming everybody down before people say a serial killer is on the loose!" I heard the nervous snapping of gum through the phone.

"That's odd. Two crimes in one day? Did someone local know the victim?"

"You don't keep up with the celebrity gossip do you? Elody Campbell is Senator Campbell's daughter. They had a huge falling out when she dropped out of college and went on the party circuit with her grungy artist boyfriend a little over a year ago. His name is Jay something or another. Anyway, he's a petty criminal who got lucky when he hooked up with Elody. An article about his artwork appeared in a big spread in a magazine. He went from drinking cheap beer at the local bar to sipping champagne with the jet setters. It was on the cover of *People Peepers* a few months ago. The Senator cut her off without a dime, but she kept on partying. It almost lost him the last election. I can't believe you didn't hear about this. You should read more than just those dusty old books in the library," Tina admonished.

Feeling chastised, I said, "You're right. I tend not to keep up with the news or gossip rags."

"The sheriff already notified the family. As soon as I saw the crime scene photos, I recognized her," Tina bragged. "At first I wasn't sure because in all the magazines she had her hair and makeup done to the max. I follow her on Twitter though, and she posted a no makeup picture of herself supporting a celebrity cause. I'm positive it was her. Her daddy may have cut her off from the family trust, but she was still living a trust fund baby's life. She went on vacations on tropical islands and dinner in Paris with that Jay guy. She tweeted about everything she did until about a month ago, then no one saw hide nor hair of her. The rumor is that she dumped him and was trying to get back in good with the family. Who knew she'd been hiding out here in Miller's Cove the whole time!"

"Thanks, Tina. I guess you didn't need my information. Between you and Nellie, the sheriff knows everything that everyone is doing. Could you let Mark know that I talked to Nicolette Simonton? Elody gave Stone Street Gallery her paintings to sell on commission. It might be nothing, but I am sure he'll want to speak to Nic. I'll chat with you later." I hung up and contemplated Tina's celebrity gossip. It was odd that a famous for being famous social butterfly would be murdered in remote Miller's Cove. We were as far removed from the nightlife of the city as you could get. My next step would be to find out as much as I could about Elody outside of the gossip pages. The only problem was how did a small town librarian with the fashion sense of a gnome learn about the hip and chic crowd of the big city?

CHAPTER SEVEN

I spent the rest of the afternoon unloading boxes of books from the van. I explained to patrons that no, I didn't know when the Founder's Day Celebration would be rescheduled, and yes, we would still hold a book sale. By the end of the day, I was grubby from the boxes and cranky from answering the same questions a dozen times. I loved the town of Miller's Cove, but the town's overactive grapevine of gossip exhausted me. Despite my protests to the contrary, everyone assumed I had all the gritty details of the investigation since I found the body. They gave me a wink and a nod hinting they understood I had to keep things under my hat. If I told them just a little nugget of gossip, they promised to stay mum. When I didn't spill the beans, they gave me a disappointed shake of their head and walked away.

When I got home, I fed Ferdie, my oversized Maine Coon cat. I poured myself a tall glass of iced tea and turned on the Philco Model 70 Cathedral radio I rescued and restored after one of my antiquing trips around the state. Soft jazz played as I strolled into my living room. I kicked off my flats and sank into my favorite chaise. With the heat of the late afternoon beating against my windows, I was grateful the prior owner had installed central air. I adored all things from the early part of the twentieth century, but I am a huge fan of cool air on a muggy summer day.

I pulled my cell phone from my front pants pocket and dialed Clint's number. His message played and the sound of his deep, husky voice sent a little thrill through my body. I left a message. "Hey you. You must still be in class. Had some excitement here today and wanted you to hear it from me first. Call me when you get a chance. Love you." I hung up and set the phone on my coffee table.

I heaved a sigh and decided I better jump in the shower before heading to the movies with Grant. The cool water washed away the day's exhaustion and book grunge. Wrapped in a towel, I picked through my closet and pulled out a navy sundress splashed with white daisies. I put on a pair of espadrilles and the small white gold heart necklace studded with blue sapphires that Clint had given me for Valentine's Day. I left my long, red curls loose around my shoulders and added a swipe of mascara and a touch of peach lip gloss. Eyeing myself in the mirror, I decided the outfit said movies with a friend and not date. After last year, I didn't want misunderstandings between Grant and me.

The doorbell rang, and I grabbed my purse and headed to the door. I stepped outside and Grant gave me a hurt look. "You won't invite me inside?"

Suppressing a nervous titter I said, "I'm ready, and I haven't been out to a movie in a long time. Let's just go." An awkward moment lay between us. The last time I watched a movie with him was right before his mother whacked me in the head with a shovel then tried to poison me. "What are we going to see?" I gave him a bright smile to hide my discomfort.

"We only have two choices. One is an action film that involved race cars and fiery explosions. You would hate it, so we're watching *African Queen.*" Grant opened the passenger door of his sports car, and I slid into the soft buttery leather seats.

"I love Katherine Hepburn. I haven't watched that movie in years. Perfect choice." This time the smile I offered him was genuine. He eased the car onto the road and ten minutes later we were pulling up to the theater.

"Listen, Phee, this isn't the time or the place, but I'm sorry for what my mother did to you and to the people here in Miller's Cove. I needed to apologize and have you forgive me before I leave. A law firm in Burlington offered me a position, and I accepted it." He pushed a hand through his blond curls.

"I don't know what to say. I understand it's hard to live here after everything that happened, but you just bought a house and started at the firm a year ago. Are you sure?"

"I've thought about it, and it would be best for everyone. The law firm has suffered because of me. To be truthful, they've been decent about the whole situation. I haven't put in enough billable hours because of all the time spent getting my mom institutionalized. Everyone looks at me and wonders if I'm like her. Next thing you know, they'll accuse me of killing the girl in the park." I tried to protest, but he put his hand up to stop me. "Phee, say what you want, but the taint of what my mother did will always follow me. Heck! I couldn't get a date with anyone here in town if I paid them."

"I'm sorry. I'm sorry that you have to leave and sorry I haven't been a friend to you through all of this." Grabbing his hand, I asked, "Forgive me?"

"Nothing to forgive. It's time for me to move on." He squeezed my hand and sat up straight. "Enough of the gloom and doom twins act. Let's go have Jujubes, slushies and one last movie together before I leave."

My eyes welled up, and I turned away. I had been a crappy friend to Grant. I had been through a lot in the past year, but friends and family surrounded me through all of it. Whenever I seemed upset or afraid, someone told me a joke, shared a cup of coffee or just sat quietly and listened. Who helped Grant? I was his closest friend. His father was dead. He had no other family. I decided even if he left, I would still try to reach out to him. I swallowed the lump in my throat, turned around and gave him a fierce hug. "I've been awful to you. There are so many things I wished I'd said, but I just…"

Grant held me and said softly, "Don't cry. I know you, and I can tell what's in your heart. It's okay. We'll be okay. Now let's stop crying and hugging before we start a rumor."

I wiped my eyes and gave a weak laugh. "That train already left the station. I'm sure rumors started when we talked in the coffee shop this morning. I'm buying the Jujubes tonight. In fact, I feel so bad about not being a good friend, I'll get you your very own box."

"Oh boy! You must feel guilty! I'm taking you up on that offer."

Two hours later, we exited the theater laughing and joking like we were teenagers. "Grant, thanks for bringing me. I'll miss you when you leave. Promise me you won't be a stranger."

"I won't. I'll come visit, and the city is just an hour away. If you feel adventurous, you could break your boycott and chat online. I swear you're the only American under thirty who doesn't use social media." Grant gave me a playful nudge. "You realize that the twenty-first century is here to stay, right?"

"Believe it or not, I'm the one who created the library's website." At Grant's incredulous look, I bragged a bit. "I can do website design. I even helped Julia with her yoga page. I just prefer to keep my personal life a little more private. The world doesn't need a status update every time I change my toenail polish!"

"Fine. We'll stick with telephone calls and smoke signals. No one in this town needs social media anyway. We've got Nellie Jo. Fastest way to hear what someone's up to is to go get a cup of coffee," Grant joked. He dropped me off and after a brief hug on the porch and a tearful "we'll keep in touch," I went inside.

It was strange that Clint hadn't returned my call. I reached into my purse to check my phone and realized I had left it on the coffee table earlier. I had five missed calls. Three were from Clint, one from my mother and one from Juliet. Listening to my messages, Clint's deep voice rumbled, "I've tried calling a couple times because I heard about the excitement in town. I'm getting a little worried. Call me when you get a chance." The next message from my mom was fishing for the latest gossip. I listened to the last message from Juliet. "Hey, PheePhee. I want to give you a head's up that Clint called me. He's a little worried that you might be upset about today. He couldn't get in touch with you, so he called to ask me to check on you. I wasn't going to tell him you went to the movies with Grant.

Clint might not have a jealous bone in his body, but he's still a man with a gun. Call him, then call me. *Ciao.*"

I groaned. I had wanted to tell him about finding the body before anyone else did. Too late now. Clint might understand me making peace with Grant, but he wouldn't like me sticking my nose into another murder.

CHAPTER EIGHT

As I started dialing Clint's number, my phone chimed out Foreigner's *Hot-Blooded*. Clint's name and number popped up on the screen. Darn Juliet for messing with my ring tones.

"Hi, Clint. Sorry for not answering earlier. I left my phone on the coffee table when I went out this evening. I've lots to tell you," I blurted.

"I was worried about you. When you didn't answer my calls earlier, I thought about jumping in my car and heading home to check on you. Jaime called to report you found Elody Campbell dead at Longfellow Park this morning. How are you holding up?" Clint asked.

I heard the concern in Clint's voice and hurried to reassure him. "This may sound weird, but I'm okay. I didn't know her, so I guess I feel a little detached. Does that make sense?"

"It does. It's always harder when you know the person. I'm glad you're okay. Jaime said it was a violent crime scene. Elody Campbell was a senator's daughter which means the FBI are making noise that they plan to take over the case for Senator Campbell's safety. Jaime is determined to run the investigation without the feds breathing down his neck. He doesn't think Elody's murder is related to the Senator or his staff."

"Tina told me that Elody is the 'it' girl on the club scene and a Tweetaholic. I suppose I should pull my head from the library stacks and read something about the famous for being famous crowd. I wonder if Audrey Hepburn would tweet if she became a star today," I mused.

"More than likely. I appreciate stars like James Dean and Bette Davis, but they had their own love-hate relationships with the press. Check out Elizabeth Taylor and all the scandal attached to her marriages. They didn't have a way to spread their gossip as quickly as stars do today. Times they are a changin', my lovely Phee." Clint sang.

"Well, aren't you the Bob Dylan wannabe!" I laughed. "So what has Jaime learned about Elody's murder that makes him think it's not related to the Senator?" *Subtle, Phee,* I thought.

"Nothing he's shared with me." Clint's voice turned serious. "I want you to leave the investigating to the professionals. After last year, I couldn't handle anything else happening to you."

"I'm just curious," I fibbed. Lying sounded so harsh. Fibs were like small half-truths. It's splitting hairs, but I didn't want him to worry about me. I twisted my hair nervously around my finger as I changed the subject. "How was your day?"

"I've been in class with our new deputy, Lu Gifford. You and I are going to have dinner with Lu Monday evening if that's okay. How's my little guy, Watson?"

"That's fine. I'll pick up a nice bottle of wine and a six-pack of beer. We can grill out. My parents are keeping Watson until tomorrow morning because I went out to the movies with Grant tonight." I slipped the last news in quickly. Juliet and Wade had planted a tiny seed of doubt in my brain this morning. It sprouted and grew flowers in the last few minutes.

"Okay." Clint drew out the word. An edge crept into his voice which made my stomach tighten.

"I ran into him at Nellie Jo's. We needed to clear the air. I'm sorry I didn't tell you beforehand, but I didn't think you would have a problem with me meeting with an old friend," I said a little defensively.

"I guess I understand," Clint said slowly. "Do you want to talk about it? You've been avoiding him, but I think it's good you finally cleared the air with Grant. You're a kind soul, Phee, and you want to save everyone. That's why I love you."

I smiled and the knot in my stomach uncoiled. "You're the sexiest, handsomest, most understanding boyfriend in the whole wide world, Clint Mason."

"I know. Can I have that engraved on a plaque so I can hang it in my office? So tell me about this evening."

"It was awkward at Nellie Jo's. Everyone was watching us. I felt like a bug under a microscope. I don't get people like Elody wanting to be watched by the public. It would freak me out. This morning wasn't the time or place for us to clear the air with people trying to eavesdrop. We went to the movies because that's always been our thing. I feel like such a jerk after we talked. Grant wasn't the reason his mom killed those people any more than I was. Everyone in town's been treating him like he's the criminal, including me. He's leaving Miller's Cove, and it's all my fault!" I wailed.

"It's not your fault. You can't blame folks for how they feel. I guarantee you that Grant understands why you've avoided him. He's not an idiot, for heaven's sake, so stop beating yourself up over it. You aren't responsible for the whole town. If you were, I'd ask for a new patrol car and a raise," Clint joked trying to lighten the mood.

"It's been one of those days. I'm tired and have a guilty conscience about Grant. I don't want it to ruin the rest of the evening though. I want to end today on a high note by flirting with a good-looking deputy on the phone." I blushed at a sudden thought. "Don't tell my mom we have phone sex!"

"I've missed you," Clint's voice lowered to a husky growl, "I don't think I've told you lately, but you're the hottest librarian I know."

"Hmm. . . I'm the only librarian you know, but it's a start," I changed my voice to what I thought was a sexy French accent. "And how are you going to make up for ze days you've been gone?"

For the next few delicious minutes, Clint told me how he planned to make me smile when he returned.

CHAPTER NINE

Ten minutes later, I hung up the phone and gave a deep sigh of contentment. My life was awesome. I had a great house, a job I loved, a close-knit family, and the man I'd been in love with since I was a gawky teenager. I leaned over and knocked on my cherry coffee table. I wasn't superstitious, but a girl could never be too careful.

I poured myself a glass of red wine and grabbed my laptop. I searched the internet for any information I could find about Elody Campbell. Page after page of gossip sites scrolled in front of me. She was breathtaking when alive. Her silvery blonde hair hung in long waves around her face. At only five feet tall, she resembled a fairy princess from Andrew Lang's *Fairy Books*.

I clicked on one of the more recent stories. "Senator's Daughter Parties with Art Scene Bad Boy" the headline announced. I read the article. "Elody Campbell was with her on-again, off-again boyfriend, Jay Burns, at Club 540 on Saturday night. Was it the lighting or was there a bruise on the lovely Elody's face? Jay Burns is the up-and-coming artist who rose from street gang obscurity to the top of the art world food chain with his pieces currently fetching five figures with Japanese collectors. Art critic, Sylvester Cline discovered him after an article in the entertainment news included photos of his work. Does Senator Campbell know his daughter parties with this artful thug whose criminal past includes assault and petty theft? Is the glazed look in her eyes from love or something else?" The article contained several images of Elody and her entourage. I clicked on one to examine it closer. Jay was attractive in a greasy way that made you take a second glance but then decide you would need to bathe him before you could kiss him. He sported silver hoops in both ears and sleeked his black hair into a ponytail. Several tattoos decorated his arms. He looked to be my age or a few years older. Definitely not my type of guy, but I could see his roguish appeal. In one photo, it looked like Elody had a bruise but with the grainy image taken in low club lights, I couldn't be sure.

I returned to my search and read through several more articles. Some hinted at drugs and wild partying by Elody and her crowd. The Senator must have had his PR team working overtime to cover up the damage his daughter's behavior caused. Reporter, Tessa Brewer, wrote most of the pieces I found. As I scanned more stories, I noticed that unlike the other reporters, Tessa's coverage of Elody seemed catty and biased. Although Tessa reported a few negative things about Jay, she mostly praised his artwork and predicted he would go far in the art world. I clicked on information about her and her column, *Celebrity Gab Rag*, and perused her coverage of other celebrities. Tessa wrote vicious barbed comments about Elody's relationship with Jay and thinly veiled accusations of drug use, but she was kinder to other celebs she covered. Maybe Tessa wanted to help sell more papers and knew Elody was the hottest club girl of the moment. Maybe she had a personal grudge against Elody. Either way, scandals and gossip sold more papers.

My cell phone blasted Prince's *Purple Rain*, the ring tone for Juliet. Ugh! "Sorry I forgot to call!"

"You're a terrible sister! I've been on pins and needles all evening waiting to find out what happened with you and Grant. Did you make up? Did he beg for forgiveness? Is Clint going to hunt him down like a wrathful warrior and avenge his woman?" Juliet drew in a deep breath and before she could continue her inquisition, I interrupted her.

"A. We made up. B. Grant said he was sorry but so am I. I've been an awful friend to him, and now he's moving away. C. Wrathful warrior? Really? Where do you get this stuff? I need to give you better books to read next time you come to the library. It sounds like a line from a regency romance. All I have to say is gross!"

"Hmmf! I'm not sorry Grant is leaving. He makes everyone uncomfortable. No one knows what to say to him. Do we ask about his mom? Do we ask how he is? It opens up a can of night crawlers and noone wants to deal with it. Clint wasn't upset? He is way too controlled with his emotions. I like my men like I like my salsa, fiery and hot," Juliet giggled. She loved Clint like a big brother, but she still liked to have a bit of drama now and then. She was in a steady relationship with Wade, so she didn't have all the man drama trauma anymore.

"I told you he wouldn't be mad, and I was right. He is amazing and perfect in every way. I've been waiting months for a horrible bad habit or tic to make him less than flawless, but. . . nada. If I lived with him, I would probably find out that he picks his toes with his dinner fork or something else disgusting, but so far, no toe pick," I said.

"You are so weird sometimes, but I love you," Juliet laughed. "Now I have an image of sitting at your kitchen table while Clint cleans his toes burned into my memory. Thanks. I won't eat dinner with you ever again."

"You are so welcome. I aim to please! I've been digging up the dirt on our victim. She's Elody Campbell, Senator Campbell's daughter."

"I heard that earlier this evening when Wade and I ate at Mimi's. It was all anyone could talk about everywhere Wade and I went," Juliet said. "I can't believe you didn't recognize her."

"Puhlease! Like I read the tabloids. I spent the evening searching the internet for recent pictures and articles about her. Did you know she dated an artist named Jay Burns? According to one article, he's a low-level thug with a criminal record. He could have killed her in a fit of passion," I theorized. I grabbed out a notepad and pen and wrote down names of the people connected to Elody.

"Maybe," Juliet agreed, "but don't jump to conclusions because of a celebrity gossip article."

"I realize that, silly. I'm the murder mystery maven of the library stacks. I'm just throwing out ideas and seeing what sticks. Possibly someone on the Senator's staff doing damage control? Or maybe the Senator himself?" I thought about the implications of Senator Campbell being a murderer. According to the political rumor mill, he planned to run for president. What lengths would he or those close to him go to ensure his nomination? I wrote his name down on my list and added Camp Campbell underneath for his staff.

"We can sit here and speculate until the owl hoots, or we could do a little investigating ourselves. I'll call the community center at the lake tomorrow and see if I can do a few yoga classes for the artists at the retreat. While I'm doing mountain pose, I can scope out our suspect pool. I'll find out what Elody was doing in Miller's Cove and who knew her," Juliet said.

"I'll go with you. I can do a little nosing around myself while we're doing yoga," I offered.

"Wait a second. Ms. I Exercise My Brain, Not My Body Jefferson is going to yoga with me?" Juliet snickered.

"I'll take the class. How hard can it be? It's not like I'll be running a marathon or anything," I sniffed. I wasn't that out of shape. I walked most places and lifting books and pushing book carts was an excellent workout. Wasn't yoga just stretching and ohming? "Let me know when to be there. In the meantime, I need sleep. I have to be at Mom and Dad's house to pick up Watson in the morning. Mom promised to make me blueberry pancakes."

"You'll need my class after Mom's pancakes and homemade whipped cream. I might sneak over and eat breakfast myself. This will be the first normal thing she's made since Dad and I began suffering through her new health kick."

"Poor Juls. I'll see you in the morning. Bye." I hung up and returned to the laptop. I looked to see if there was any contact information for reporter Tessa Brewer. I should call and ask what her connection was to Elody. I glanced at the clock above my stove. It was close to ten on a Saturday night, so there was zero chance I could track Tessa down tonight. It would have to wait until Monday morning.

I yawned and gave Ferdie a scratch behind the ears. Time for bed. I hoped I would dream about Clint and not a dead girl in a park.

CHAPTER TEN

The next morning I drove to my parent's house for blueberry pancakes. My mother was a phenomenal cook, but she and Dad recently started a weird longevity diet involving nuts, berries and seeds. At least this was Juliet's claim as she bemoaned, "Mom's making Dad and me eat squirrel food." Juliet didn't cook, so she grazed at other people's houses as often as she could.

I opened the front door to my parent's house and called out to them. Watson bounded up on his short little legs and wiggled his nubby tail and butt with joy. "Hi boy! Did you miss me? Did you'ums have a doggie play date?" I picked him up, and he licked my face.

"Good morning, sweetheart. Watson was on his best behavior. I think this was the first time he didn't dig around the yard and drag any dead thing he found up to the house." Mom scratched him behind the ear. "Speaking of dead, I wasn't two feet inside the door of the church this morning before three people came up to weasel information out of me. I told them it wouldn't be right for me to gossip at church. The look on their faces was priceless. No one will ask me to lunch for the foreseeable future. You would think after last year, people would have had their fill of crime! The whole town is whispering about Senator Campbell and poor Elody. Such a waste." She shook her head.

"I'm sorry, Mom. I wish somebody else had found her. Jaime will catch the killer, then everything can return to normal. Thanks for watching Watson for me. Grant and I talked and made peace although it might be too late to save our friendship. He plans to leave Miller's Cove."

"Well, honey, I can't blame him. If it was me, I would have left right after everything happened. I'm glad you spent some time with him. You've been friends for too long to not talk. Come into the kitchen while I finish making breakfast. Your dad took Hamlet for a jog. He should be back soon."

"Dad's jogging? Really? Why?" My parents were retired academics, not athletes. Both slim and healthy, they spent most of their time outdoors in the garden, playing tennis or hiking. A new diet and now jogging? Something was fishy in the Parental Palace.

"Your father had his yearly physical a few weeks ago," Mom rinsed the blueberries in a colander. "It's nothing to worry about but his blood pressure and cholesterol were a little higher than normal. We decided it's time we took better care of ourselves. We're getting older, so things require more maintenance than they used to."

"Juliet whined about your nuts and berries diet," I said. "I think it's a good thing you're eating healthy. I want you and dad around for a long time." I walked over to the sink and gave my mom a quick hug. She leaned over and kissed me on my forehead.

"Well, I don't plan on croaking for quite some time. I want to see grandkids from you and Juliet before I'm eighty! Your brother and the twins should be here any minute. Rick called and said Carrie needed a mommy break, so he is bringing Zoe and Sam over for a visit." She pulled a pitcher of juice from the refrigerator. "Put this on the table, please."

"Juliet plans to drop in, too. I let it slip you were fixing blueberry pancakes. Juls won't pass on a meal she didn't have to cook herself." I pulled dishes from the cupboard and set the table. The kitchen door opened and Dad walked in with Hamlet, followed by Rick and the babies. I grabbed a baby carrier from Rick as he struggled through the door.

"Shh… I just got them to sleep. Help me put them in the bedroom. Juliet's pulling into the driveway. Quiet is not a word she knows, so I want to get them settled before she gets in here." Rick set the twins' diaper bag on the floor. He walked down the hallway towards his old room. It was no longer covered with baseball pictures and sports trophies from Rick's glory days in high school. The walls had been transformed into a magical painted forest with bunnies and squirrels scampering through the grass and birds soaring through the fluffy clouds. Mom had outdone herself decorating the room for her first grandbabies.

Picking up Zoe, I gazed down at her pink, chubby cheeks. I watched her rosebud lips quiver with each little soft snore. I wanted to hold her close and inhale her sweet baby scent. A sudden wave of longing for a child of my own swept through me. After I kissed her cheek, I laid her down in her crib. Rick tucked Sam into his crib. We tiptoed out of the room. Rick shut the door behind us.

As I walked into the kitchen, I overheard Juliet exclaim, "Oh my gosh! You would not believe the craziness downtown! It was like a three-ring circus getting out of my apartment and to my car." Juliet lived above an antique store in a small one-bedroom apartment. "It's a paparazzi explosion and you would think Queen Elizabeth arrived in town the way everyone acts. Nellie was so busy she made Mike put on an apron and serve coffee."

"You knew it would happen as soon as the press got wind that Elody Campbell was the victim," I said. Everyone sat down at the table to eat. I speared a piece of blueberry pancake and dipped it into the inky purple syrup pooling on my plate. I took a bite and stopped. "Mom, something's wrong with my pancakes. They taste...don't take this wrong, weird."

"Your mother is making me eat ungodly gluten-free, sugar-free, enjoyment-free food," Dad grumbled as he stuffed pancake in his mouth and swallowed it. "If I die, it'll be from this Frankenfood stuff she's serving me, not a little cholesterol. At least if I ate a steak, I'd die happy and full." He sipped his coffee and grimaced. "Decaf."

"It's for your own good." Mom gave him an injured look. "Phee, I made the pancakes with a blend of coconut and bean flours. You'll get used to it. It's healthy and nutritious. It won't kill you."

"Told ya," Juliet snorted under her breath. She took a sip of orange juice. "I hope all these reporters don't plan on taking up permanent residence downtown. We might have to rent out rooms at your house, Phee."

"It will die down in a day or two." I put down my fork. I wasn't hungry for bluefrankenberry pancakes. If this was Mom's idea of food, we'd be eating tofurkey for our next holiday meal. "How's Carrie doing, Rick?"

"She's tired. Both Zoe and Sam are teething and miserable. I do what I can, but I've got an important project going at work. I'm working sixty hours a week to finish it. Carrie deserves a break, so I'm having a daddy day with the twins and came over to enjoy Mom's great cooking." Rick took a big bite and gulped it down. He gave Mom a bright smile.

"Kiss up," Juliet whispered. I choked back a giggle.

"Thank you, Rick," Mom beamed at him. "At least one child appreciates me."

"I appreciate you, Mom." I picked up my fork. After two attempts, I swallowed the gummy, bean-flavored concoction. "It's good!"

"Phee, I set up the yoga class at the lake's recreation center for tomorrow morning. It's short notice, but it starts at six. You'll still have time to get ready for work afterwards. It'll be fun," Juliet winked at me. Rick frowned at us both and shook his head. My exercise abhorrence was no secret, so he knew Juliet and I were up to shenanigans.

"I'd love to go. If Dad can jog, I can yogi… yoga… yogic… whatever. You know what I mean. We'll be healthy together," I crossed my fingers and hoped my butt didn't expand two sizes for my lie. While Juliet loosened everyone's muscles with her mountain pose, I'd loosen their tongues about Elody and why someone took her life.

CHAPTER ELEVEN

I waddled out to Velma. Watson panted with excitement at the prospect of going for a ride. My guilt over criticizing Mom's healthy pancakes made me eat two servings. I felt like an overripe blueberry ready to burst. I heaved myself into the van and vowed to try one of Juliet's wacky cleansing juice fasts the next day to recover.

I decided to check out all the hoopla with the press. As I turned on to Oakwyn Street by Longfellow Park, I slowed Velma to a crawl. Juliet hadn't exaggerated. There wasn't one parking spot as far as I could see. News vans with station logos and mini satellite dishes on top and cars with out-of-state tags littered the side streets around the park. One enterprising soul even parked their van on the sidewalk. I pulled into a space a few blocks from the entrance. After clipping a leash on Watson, I walked over to a gaggle of paparazzi pushing and craning their necks to get a view of the crime scene. A microphone was set up in the band shell. Sheriff Dawes stood talking in close quarters with a red-haired man in an expensive suit. Behind them stood Senator Campbell and a young, pony-tailed guy who had to be Jay Burns. Senator Campbell ignored Jay as he surveyed the jostling crowd of reporters. Clearly, there was no love lost between the Senator and his daughter's wayward boyfriend.

The sheriff stepped to the microphone and tapped it with his finger. "Is this thing on?" The speakers let out a high-pitched squeal. He cleared his throat and tried again. "Ladies and gentlemen, I'll read a short statement before turning this over to Senator Campbell. We won't field questions from the press today. The body of Elody Campbell, daughter of Senator Richard Campbell, was discovered early yesterday morning here in Longfellow Park. Miss Campbell was the victim of foul play and the Miller's Cove Sheriff's Department is working around the clock to solve this heinous crime. Preliminary results from the autopsy indicate an unknown suspect shot her at close range with a .22 caliber weapon. We're in the early stages of the investigation and pursuing several lines of inquiry. Now I'll turn things over to Senator Campbell's aide, Anthony Ziegfried."

"Sheriff Dawes! Who discovered the body?" A female reporter shouted.

"Again, no questions. Mr. Ziegfried will give a brief statement." Sheriff Dawes mouth was a hard line brooking no argument. He stepped back from the microphone, and the red-haired man in the suit stepped forward. "The Senator, his family and friends are saddened and shocked by Elody's murder. Elody was the light of the Senator's life and a bright beacon of talent and hope has been extinguished too soon. The Senator lost his beloved wife, Patsy, three years ago to cancer. Now, his only child has been brutally murdered. The Senator plans to examine our current gun laws and fight to make our state safer for our children. He is offering a $50,000 reward to information leading to the capture and conviction of the individual who killed Elody." A sob rang out from the stage. Jay Burns buried his face in his hands. He cried, letting out loud donkey brays of anguish. Senator Campbell shot him a disgusted glare and stepped to the microphone.

"Ladies and gentlemen, I will do everything in my power to find the person who did this to my beautiful daughter. I won't stop until I make sure that every citizen in this fine state of ours is guaranteed a safe home free from crime. Please allow me the opportunity to mourn in private. There is a candlelight vigil for Elody here tonight. It's open to the press and public. A funeral for family and close friends will take place in my hometown at a later date." He stepped back from the microphone. After giving a curt nod to the sheriff, he strode off the stage. Anthony Ziegfried galloped after him.

"Well, that was a load of crap if I ever heard it," a voice drawled next to me. I turned and saw a young woman with multiple facial piercings and dreadlocks glaring at the retreating Senator's back.

"Pardon?" I said.

"It's baloney. I can't believe the Senator used Elody's murder for his campaign platform. He cut her off without a dime because she went a little wild after her mom died. And Jay Burns gets the Horse Hockey of the Year award. He's crying and carrying on about Elody, but every time she turned her back, he cozied up to other women." She gave a disgusted snort. "The only thing they got right was she was beautiful and too young to die."

"Sorry, but I didn't catch your name. Mine's Phee. You and Elody were friends?" I asked while gaging if this girl was a crackpot fan of the quasi-famous or an actual friend.

"Sorry. I'm Willow. I met her about a month ago when she came to our artist's retreat, but we had a real connection. I mean, like, I understood that her spirit felt harmed by all the negativity from the press, her dad, her loser boyfriend…from everyone. She was getting to a good place here. Really getting in touch with her inner awesomeness as a child of Mother Earth." Willow touched a large stone she wore on a silver chain around her neck to her lips and raised it to the sky.

"Okay," I said slowly. I was dealing with a little package of crazy here. "So you're an artist, too?"

"I help the artists channel their creative vibe - a conduit between the earth, the sky and their artistic soul. I cleanse their auras so their art can be pure."

"For real?" I asked not masking my disbelief. "How do you do that?" Juliet would eat this chick up and take her home to be her new roomie if they ever met.

"You don't believe me?" Willow gave me a pitying look. "You experienced great strife in the past year. A dark spirit hovers near you stealing your light. Focus on you and stop giving away all your energy to everyone else."

I gave her a wide-eyed stare of amazement. Maybe she could read my aura. Getting whacked in the head with a shovel by a crazed matchmaking mama counted as strife. I gathered my courage to ask her how to cleanse the darkness, but Juliet bounded up to us and interrupted.

"Hey, Phee. I see you've met Willow. Isn't she awesome?" Juliet burbled. She reached down and gave Watson a friendly scratch behind his ears. I should have realized Juliet and Willow were friends. They both spouted the same New Age woo woo feel good words.

"She's something else," I commented dryly. Now I understood why Willow saw strife in my aura. Juliet told her all about her big sister Phee and her near-death experience. "Did you realize Willow was friends with Elody?"

"Sure! We met this morning when we were both fighting the mad mob to get coffee. I forgot to tell you about it. Willow, I guess you figured out this was my sister."

"Yeah. I just read her aura. You didn't tell me she had a dark smudge on it. You and I should put our collective spirits together to heal her." Willow turned to me and said, "If you want us to do it. The spirits guide me to heal, but not everyone accepts the spirits' gifts."

"I'll consider it. I'm a down-to-earth girl, and I don't know if I believe in auras, tarot cards and spirits. No offense."

"No problem. So, Juls, I'll see you at yoga tomorrow morning. It's righteous of you to offer the class. The spirits appreciate your gift. Glad to meet a fellow yogi. Peace." Willow walked away with her long purple skirt swirling around her ankles.

"I am so excited I met someone who cleanses auras!" Juliet exclaimed doing a jig of joy.

"Me, too," I responded not bothering to mask my sarcasm. "Just what I need. Two hippie dippy chicks in my life. Did you hear Jaime say Elody was shot? I knew there was something fishy about that paintbrush buried in her chest. The killer wanted to mislead the police or destroy evidence. Maybe whoever killed her is a crazed person making an artistic statement. A fellow artist from the retreat in a fit of jealousy shot her then made her his final masterpiece."

"You're flinging out crazy theories again, Phee. They say I'm the flighty, imaginative sister? Ha! Did you see Jay Burns crying and creating a big scene? We should come for the memorial service tonight. We can dig up some dirt. We might even weasel information out of Jay. Are you in?" Juliet asked.

"Like Flynn. Meet me at my house and we'll walk over. Parking will be a nightmare with the hyenas sniffing around for a news story."

"Later alligator."

"After a while, crocodile," I shot back as Watson and I headed for home and a little more online snooping.

CHAPTER TWELVE

I went home and fed Ferdie and Watson. I needed cat food for Ferdie and heaven forbid his pantry ever ran low. It was a glorious summer day, so I hopped on my vintage turquoise Schwinn with the cute basket on the front and biked downtown. Most stores in Miller's Cove stayed closed on Sunday, but Abe's Supermarket opened at noon. Baskets sat inside the front door, so I grabbed one and headed for the pet food aisle. As I made my way past the fresh fruits and vegetables, I spotted a woman who resembled the pictures I saw last night of Tessa Brewer yakking on her cell phone. Ambling by the bananas, I perused the produce to get a closer look.

"I tell you, Amber, I'm stuck in the backwoods of hell," the woman complained to someone on the other end of the line. "Ask for sushi and they stare at you like you grew a second head. The guy at the dive diner where I ate lunch brought me a fried fish sandwich. I got up and walked out without paying. I can't wait to return to civilization. After this week, I'm treating myself to a day at the spa."

I couldn't hear what the other person was saying, but I moved closer and gave a side glance at the woman on the phone – definitely Tessa Brewer. Her online photo didn't do her justice. An attractive brunette, she was short with a slim, athletic build. If I wasn't mistaken, she wore a dress by Coco Chanel . I might not be fashion savvy, but I recognized a classic when I saw it. Unfortunately, I can't afford designer anything on my librarian's salary. I never realized reporters made the kind of money Tessa must have to afford her wardrobe. Besides the Chanel suit, she sported a Louis Vuitton bag on her arm.

"Amber, you should see all these idiots crying over Elody. I guarantee none of them ever met her. Just a bunch of star-crushers hoping to get their picture in the gossip columns. Mark my words. Elody Campbell's murder will push me into the big leagues. No more running around after self-centered, vapid trust fund babies. If I play my cards right, I'll land a sweet deal at the *Times*. Might even snare the crime beat." Tessa pushed her shopping cart over to the tomatoes. She picked them up and inspected them one at a time. "I'll talk to you later. I need to find some local yokel to track down a real tomato." She closed her phone and dropped it into her bag.

"Excuse me. Do you work here?" Tessa said to me.

"No. Why? Is there something you need help with? I can go grab Abe. He owns the market and is running around somewhere," I offered. I grabbed a head of lettuce to disguise the fact I'd been spying on her.

"I want a decent tomato, not this crap they're selling. Where are the organic, heirloom tomatoes?" Tessa slammed the tomato she held on the bin splitting the skin. Juice and seeds shot out and spotted her dress. "That's just great! I give up. I don't understand how you people live without the basic amenities. Might as well be pioneers." She left her cart and marched out of the market in a huff.

"That woman is a pain in my you know what," Abe said from behind me. "I was right around the corner, but there was no way I wanted to come out and talk to her. She came in here yesterday evening wanting some kind of weird fruit.

She claimed she ate one every morning for breakfast, but they didn't serve it at the B&B. When I told her I'd never even heard of it let alone sold it, she complained about backwoods and hillbillies." Abe picked up the squashed tomato. His grizzled beard bristled in outrage. Abe inherited the market from his dad, Abe Sr., twenty years before I was born. This market was the cornerstone of our small village, and we loved Abe and his wife, Shannon. Tessa Brewer was a bully.

"Well, I like your tomatoes just fine. They're perfect for the salad I'm fixing tomorrow." I grabbed several and put them in my basket. Feeling guilty over Tessa's behavior, I picked up five more. I'd give some to Mrs. Lassiter, my next door neighbor.

"You're a peach, Phee. Folks like that have something broken in them making them act like a horse's behind to the rest of us." Abe turned away to finish cleaning up the mess. I returned to my quest for Ferdie's kibbles.

When I arrived home twenty minutes later, I set a few tomatoes on the windowsill to ripen. Ferdie sensed it was all about him in the grocery bags. I swear he could smell cat food from a mile away. He'd weigh a hundred pounds if I wasn't in control of his diet. I placed an open brown sack onto the floor and he squeezed his fat rear in and lay down. His tail twitched against the side and made the bag rattle. Ferdie loved his hidey-holes.

I made myself a glass of tea and decided to find out more about Tessa Brewer. Maybe she had a rich husband or family to fund her expensive wardrobe. I opened a browser and searched for her name. Thousands of hits populated my screen. Scrolling through them, I saw most were from her byline as a reporter. I cleared my search and went to my library's website. I clicked our online database link and searched for Tessa Brewer and excluded her gossip column and recent items. Bingo! Librarians are the smarter more efficient search engine.

I clicked on an article from fifteen years ago. Tessa looked to be my age, so she was a teenager when this was written. It came from a small newspaper published somewhere in Arkansas. I read through the article and when I finished, I whistled in surprise. Tessa Brewer had certainly recreated herself if what I read was true.

CHAPTER THIRTEEN

I walked next door to Mrs. Lassiter's house with two tomatoes in my hand. An elegant woman in her eighties, Joan Lassiter was the town matriarch. Her approval guaranteed success for any project planned by the town council. Mrs. Lassiter wasn't only my neighbor. She served as president of the Friends of the Miller's Cove Library, so I stayed on her good side. I kept my hedges trimmed and mowed my grass before she could cast a critical eye on it. She sat on the front porch on a wicker chaise lounge sipping a tall glass of lemonade.

"What a pleasant surprise. Come sit down and tell me what in the world is going on with Founder's Day." Mrs. Lassiter gestured towards the chair beside her. "I already heard about the murder in the park. Phee, nice young ladies do not stumble on dead bodies willy nilly like you do. You need to settle down with that handsome Clint Mason and start a family. Leave the criminals to the police."

"Yes, ma'am. I'm happy to let the sheriff handle murders and mayhem. I went to the park to set up the tables for the book sale. Sometimes the early bird doesn't catch a tasty worm," I gave her my best humble smile of apology. Mrs. Lassiter had used her influence to convince, although some would say bully, the town council to fund a remodel of the library next year. I was not above kowtowing. The library needed new shelves.

"I understand, dear. I'm sure if that Sheriff Dawes spent more time patrolling and less time behind the desk, this crime wave wouldn't have happened. He might even lose a little of that belly he sucks in every time he talks at the council meetings," Mrs. Lassiter pursed her lips in a moue of distaste.

"The victim was Senator Campbell's daughter, Elody," I informed her. "There's a memorial service tonight at the park for her."

"I knew Richard Campbell when he was a child. His mother and I attended university together. Ladies went to college to earn their M R S degree back in my day." Seeing my puzzlement, she explained, "We went to college to catch a husband, dear. None of us planned to work. The goal was to marry a nice, young man from a good family."

"What was Mr. Lassiter like?" I asked her. She had one picture of her husband from their wedding day. It hung over the mantel of the living room fireplace. He had a studious face. Mrs. Lassiter was gorgeous in her youth. Like they said in my favorite classic movies, a real pip.

"George was quiet and kind. To look at him, you'd wonder what I saw in him. He had the most beautiful singing voice though. It was his singing that won my heart. He used to stare at me over his book at the library. I always pretended not to notice. One day I was with my girlfriends in the university cafeteria when George walked up with a single white rose and sang to me. I fell in love with him that day and we married a year later."

"What did he sing?" I asked. I loved romantic gestures. Clint loved me but was way too practical for flowers and songs.

"He sang *Only You* by The Platters. It became our song. I shocked my mother and insisted they play it for the first dance at our wedding. George was the only man for me." She stared off into the distance as she remembered a day long ago.

"What happened to George, Mrs. Lassiter? You never talk about him," I probed. I wanted to hear about their romance and life together.

"He died less than a year into our marriage," Mrs. Lassiter said in a sad voice. "His head was in the clouds all the time. Kind of like a young lady, I know. We married our senior year at university. We decided to delay our honeymoon and make it a combined graduation and marriage celebration trip. He and I went to Maine two weeks after graduation. George was an avid birdwatcher. He spotted some endangered bird and followed it. He walked right off a cliff and drowned. I hope the damned bird is extinct! Sorry, dear. I didn't mean to say a curse word. It broke my heart losing George. I vowed to never love another man again." She took a long sip from her glass. "Enough being a Gloomy Gertie, young lady. I plan to attend this memorial service tonight. I need to talk to young Richard and see if he grew into a man who would make his mother proud."

"I should be going. I need to fix dinner and change clothes before this evening. If it wouldn't be too much trouble, could you introduce me to the Senator?" Mrs. Lassiter could be my entrance into Camp Campbell.

"It's not a problem. I'm calling his mother now. She's retired to Florida to an old folk's home where the nurses make you do senior chair aerobics and all sorts of foolishness. You won't catch me dead in a place like that," she said firmly. "I plan on dying in my own home."

"Don't talk like that, Mrs. Lassiter. I don't want anything to happen to you," I insisted. She might be prickly, but I loved her. I grew teary-eyed thinking of her gone.

"You're a sweet girl, Phee. A good girl. Settle down and marry that young man. I want to hold your children on my lap before I leave this world," Mrs. Lassiter said as she patted me on my hand. "I think I'll lie down for a nap after I call Kitty Campbell. It will take all my energy to deal with this evening's service."

"I'll see you tonight," I said and walked down her porch steps. On my way back to my house, I considered my wardrobe choices for the evening. What did one wear to a memorial service and an interrogation of a senator? I didn't know, but I bet no book on etiquette ever addressed this fashion dilemma.

I fixed myself a salad for dinner, then dived into my closet to look for an outfit. Thirty minutes later, I decided a black sleeveless dress with flat sandals and pearls fit the bill. If Nancy Drew lived, she would adore my outfit. I tried to channel her spirit and style, but Miss Marple was the only one who answered. Large frumpy hats and Peter Pan collars wouldn't cut it this evening.

"Hello! Pheeble Mind! Are you here?" Juliet called.

I wanted to travel back in time and tell my parents to please pick another name, any name, other than Ophelia. My nicknames ranged from Flea, PheePhee, Oph, and now this latest addition, Pheeble Mind. I silently praised Carrie every day for choosing Zoe and Samuel for the twins' names.

"No one by that name lives here. If you're looking for the amazing, the beautiful, the brilliant Super Librarian, then here I am," I responded. I walked out of my bedroom strutting like a Paris runway model. "Don't hate. Just appreciate."

Juliet whistled. "You look good for someone going to a memorial service in the park. What's up with the fancy duds?"

"This isn't fancy. If you owned anything besides yoga pants and blue jeans, you would realize I am simply wearing an appropriate frock for fraternizing with Senator Campbell. Mrs. Lassiter said she would introduce me to him tonight at the service. She went to college with his mother, Kitty Campbell," I informed Juliet. "While I'm schmoozing with the bigwigs, you can get close to Jay and see what you can find out from him."

"Great. I get the dirty artist and you meet a senator. Why do I always get stuck with the grungy guys?" Juliet pouted.

"Really? You dated a man for two months who lived in a tent and made his living singing on a street corner begging for change. You don't even own a pair of heels. You have a tattoo of a polar bear on your behind from one date with Tattoo Bob. Do I need to continue?" I had plenty more dating disaster scenarios from Juliet's life.

Juliet bared her teeth at me and meowed. "Catty much? I did those things when I was young and dumb. I've matured."

"It was two years ago. Case closed. Do not pass go. Do not collect two hundred dollars," I informed her.

"Fine. Wade's good for me. He civilizes and calms my inner wild child," Juliet said. She plopped onto my couch and kicked off her flip flops. She rested her feet on my coffee table. I glared at the offending electric blue polished toenails.

"I found out something interesting today. It involves crime, doing time, and the reporter Tessa Brewer," I said as I sat primly on the other side of the sofa and inspected my nails. I whistled and waited.

"What? I want to hear all about it," Juliet dropped her feet from the table and sat forward to listen.

Mission accomplished. Feet secured to the floor. "Tessa Brewer was an accomplice in an armed robbery when she was sixteen years old."

"What the heck? Are you kidding me? Details, Phee. I want all the juicy details," Juliet practically panted like a puppy in her eagerness to hear my news.

"On one condition. You never call me Pheeble Mind again."

"Fine. People have no sense of humor. It isn't my fault Mom and Dad gave you a name begging for mockery. So what's the word, nerd?"

"Tessa was the getaway driver for her own father. Truth is stranger than fiction. She and her father pulled a string of armed robberies all over Arkansas. Turns out, that's where she lived before moving to this state. Her dad shot a man during a hold-up at a convenience store in some podunk town. The police caught them, and Tessa was almost tried as an adult. Her defense attorney argued her deadbeat dad made her drive the car. Since the dad was her only living family member, the judge took pity on her. He sentenced her to a juvenile facility until her eighteenth birthday. After her release, she fell off the radar screen until about four years ago when she began writing a gossip column for the newspaper."

"Holy jalapeños! A convicted robber right here in our midst. We need to meet Tessa and question her. She has a criminal mind already. I just moved her onto our suspect list," Juliet declared. If she had a badge and a gun, my sister would be lethal. Lethal with her 1970s cop lingo, that is.

"I met her. She reinvented herself better than a prisoner turned preacher. She wears Coco Chanel and designer shoes. No southern accent and she has the attitude of a spoiled socialite from the Hamptons. She threw a hissy fit in Abe's today over a tomato because it wasn't heirloom and organic. You're right about one thing. She has a criminal mind. She killed one of Abe's tomatoes right in the produce aisle with her bare hands!"

CHAPTER FOURTEEN

Juliet and I walked to Longfellow Park fifteen minutes before the start of the memorial service. We weren't the only ones curious about the events unfolding in our small village. The majority of the town crowded the small park. Between the news reporters, townsfolk, and people arriving from out of town for the service, Miller's Cove had never seen so much action. Our sleepy hamlet was now a bustling metropolis and murder was the cause.

I spotted Nellie Jo and Mike milling around near the band shell. I lifted my hand and waved. Juliet and I shouldered our way through the masses until we made our way to where they stood. "Nellie Jo, I knew I'd find you here," I said.

"Why me and Mike wouldn't miss a big event like this. I got my autograph book with me. I plan on meeting a movie star or somebody famous tonight." Nellie Jo showed us the bright red autograph book she held in her hand.

"I didn't realize they made autograph books still," I said.

"I've had this book since I was a little girl. Look here. I've got an autograph from Rowdy Rick. He was famous in the seventies in the wrestling ring. I even got Boots Chavez, the famous zydeco musician. One day this here little book is gonna be worth a ton of money," Nellie Jo proclaimed. Mike rolled his eyes. Mike was as gray as Nellie Jo was colorful. A quiet man, he spent his time working at his pickle factory and rarely ventured into town. From conversations with Nellie in the past, I knew Mike collected guns and didn't care for the federal government too much. According to Nellie, Mike ranted about the government trying to control his pickle brine with too many "dag burn regulations."

"I don't know how many celebrities will be here tonight," Juliet said. "It will mostly be Elody's groupies and the press."

"I don't care. If they look famous, I'm gonna get them to sign my book," Nellie Jo declared.

"Mrs. Lassiter is trying to get my attention. Nice seeing you and Mike. If I spot any celebrities I'll send them your way," I promised. "Juliet, I'll meet up with you at the fountain in an hour. You've got your assignment."

"Yeah yeah. I'm on the case." Juliet turned and worked her way through the crowd searching for her quarry, Jay Burns.

It took me five minutes to arrive at Mrs. Lassiter's side. The disgruntled frown on her face told me what she thought about the crowds. "Sorry. It's a madhouse. I'm surprised I didn't get a black eye fighting my way here. You would think we were at a rock concert instead of a memorial service," I said. I straightened my skirt and tried smoothing my curls.

"It's a spectacle and a crying shame. A girl died and the vultures immediately start circling." Mrs. Lassiter shook her head in disgust. "My George would roll in his grave if he had lived to see what our world's become."

"You're right. I'll stick with my dusty books. They are much better than the gossip rags fueling this bunch," I replied.

"Of course I'm right," Mrs. Lassiter harrumphed. "Richard said an Anthony Ziegfried would come get us. He was to be here five minutes ago."

"He's probably trapped by paparazzi. I'm sure the press recognized him the minute he arrived with the Senator. Like you said, vultures," I said trying to soothe her ruffled feathers. Mrs. Lassiter had no patience for lack of punctuality or bad manners.

A moment later, a red head bobbed its way through the masses. When he made his way to our side, he was out of breath. "Ladies, I apologize. It's a madhouse. Half these people never even heard of Elody until now."

Anthony Ziegfried exuded confidence and success. He possessed the polished good looks of an Ivy League education. Bright blue eyes gleamed with intelligence behind stylish frames and his charcoal gray suit cost more than I earned in a month. "I'm Ophelia Jefferson. Mrs. Lassiter is my neighbor," I introduced myself.

"A fellow ginger! Nice to meet you. Anthony Ziegfried, aide to the Senator, errand boy, chauffeur and anything else the occasion may need." Anthony's handshake was firm and his manner friendly and easy going. My nervousness at meeting the Senator eased.

"Ophelia discovered poor Elody's body. She shouldn't have been in the park at the crack of dawn, but she handled it well. No hysterics and she kept the public away until the sheriff took control of the scene," Mrs. Lassiter said.

"Ah. The sheriff told us the town librarian discovered Elody. From what I understand, you were setting up for the Founder's Day Celebration," Anthony smoothed over Mrs. Lassiter's disapproval of my presence in the park. "Senator Campbell wants to speak with you alone for a few minutes about what you saw when you found her."

"Didn't the sheriff tell him the details?" I asked. I didn't want to describe the horrible scene to Elody's father.

"The Senator wants to hear it straight from the horse's mouth, so to speak," Anthony said. "He is well aware of how sanitized the reports to the victim's family can be. Richard Campbell is a straight-shooter. Don't worry about sparing his feelings. Give him the unvarnished truth."

"I don't know how much I can add, but I'll talk to him," I agreed. A heavy cloud settled over me at the thought of sharing the details of the scene with the Senator.

"If you would both like to follow me, I'll take you to the Senator. The service should start in ten minutes, so we need to hustle," Anthony instructed us. He guided Mrs. Lassiter around the back of the shell to where Senator Campbell stood flanked by two women in business suits. When he spotted us, he broke off his conversation and walked to Mrs. Lassiter and hugged her. "Aunt Joan, thank you for coming."

"Richard, I'm sorry for your loss. I know how hard it's been for you since Patsy's death and now this. If I can do anything for you, please call me." Mrs. Lassiter grasped his hand between her two wrinkled ones. The Senator's face softened and lost its public demeanor. Here was the face of a father, not a politician, worn down by too much grief in too few years. I felt guilty for suspecting him even for a second of his daughter's murder.

I stepped forward to express my condolences. "Senator Campbell, I'm Ophelia Jefferson. I'm sorry about your daughter's death. I'm the person who found her in the park on Saturday."

"Thank you, Ms. Jefferson. I wanted to speak to you but in a more private setting. Could you come to dinner at our summer cabin tomorrow evening?" Senator Campbell asked.

"Certainly, Senator. I doubt I have much to add to what the sheriff told you, but I'm willing to answer any questions." Even though it would be uncomfortable to share what I found, dinner with him would allow me to discover more information about Elody.

"Call me Richard, please. Anthony will give you directions to the cabin. I'll see you at six sharp tomorrow evening. Now if you'll excuse me, I need to discuss a few more things with my staff before the service starts. Aunt Joan, I'll call you tomorrow and make plans for a visit."

"Fine, Richard. I'll speak to you soon," Mrs. Lassiter said with a regal nod of her head.

Reverend Taylor walked to the microphone. He tapped it several times with his finger to make sure it worked. He cleared his throat and asked everyone to bow their heads as he offered a prayer for Elody. When the prayer ended, I opened my eyes. In front of me, I saw Tessa Brewer leaning in close to talk to Nicolette Simon. I might as well ferret out some more information from our criminal-turned-girl reporter.

CHAPTER FIFTEEN

By the time I made my way to where they stood, Nicolette had left. I sidled up next to Tessa. I pretended to listen to Reverend Taylor's homily, but I watched Tessa from the corner of my eye. She didn't even glance at the stage. Instead, she texted someone, her nails flying across the small screen.

I turned towards her and said, "You were at the market today, weren't you?"

Not bothering to look up, Tessa shrugged. "I was there, but I shouldn't have bothered. The place is a dump."

"Were you friends with Elody?" I ignored her snide remark about Abe's. I had bigger fish to fry.

"Was I friends with Elody? Hmm...let's see," Tessa said. She finally looked up and fixed her steely-blue gaze on me. "I knew Elody better than most people here pretending to mourn her. I knew the real Elody. The one who partied until four in the morning and used everyone in her circle of friends for money when dear old daddy cut off access to her trust fund."

I hid my shock at the venom in her voice. "Sounds like you didn't care for her too much. Wait a minute. Aren't you Tessa Brewer? I read your articles all the time!" I gushed and twisted one of my red curls in my fingers. I yanked my hand down quickly to stop my nervous tic. "So what was she like?"

"She was shallow and self-centered. She hung on Jay Burns and relied on his caché with the art world to keep her face in the news. Kind of pathetic if you ask me. I'm sure daddy's staffers are thrilled they don't have to hide her escapades from us anymore," Tessa said with a snide twist of her lip.

"You must be glad to not cover Elody's party circuit anymore. I love your writing. You should write the crime beat. You would be amazing!" I made my voice high and breathy like I imagined a fan's would sound.

Preening like a peacock, Tessa smiled. "I talked to my editor about a possible move to the crime beat yesterday. Watch for my name to appear in the byline of the Crime Time column in the near future. It was nice meeting you…what did you say your name was?"

"Phee. It's an honor to meet you. I can't wait to read your column in the crime section," I gave her a wide, toothy grin. I'm positive I looked like a rabid raccoon who slammed caffeine drinks twenty-four seven.

"Got to run. Photo ops abound with Senator Campbell taking the stage. Ta for now." She wiggled her fingers at me and threaded her way to the band shell.

I glanced down at my watch and realized I'd be late to meet Juliet if I didn't step on it. I pushed my way through the crowd to the fountain. Juliet wasn't there yet. Juliet was tall, so it was easy to spot her long, blonde hair in the sea of faces. I scanned the crowd and spotted her talking to Jay Burns. She leaned in close to Jay to tell him something. From this angle, it looked as if she were whispering in his ear. They stood talking until a few bright flashes from a paparazzo's camera startled them. Juliet stepped back from Jay then sprinted towards me. A few more flashes of the camera captured her fleeing back.

When she arrived at the fountain, she fumed, "Oh my goddess! Did you see that jerk photographer take my picture? I could never deal with this every day. What an invasion of privacy. Makes me rethink my love of the gossip magazines."

"You do realize you'll end up on the front page of a scandal sheet by tomorrow morning?"

"I doubt it. Too many other interesting people to watch. I made contact with our subject," Juliet said in her best cop voice.

"I saw. I met the Senator. He invited me to dinner tomorrow night. He wants to talk about Elody," I reported.

"Cool pickles. We are on fire with our investigating skills tonight. Jay invited you and me to lunch tomorrow. We'll meet him at one o'clock at Odd Couple's. He wanted to see me alone later tonight, but I begged off and told him I had to meet with you. It was like shooting fish in a pickle barrel. He is a man who thinks with his libido, not with his brain."

"Good job. I also ran into Tessa Brewer. She didn't mince her words when it came to Elody. We should try to talk to a few more people while we're here. I doubt we'll have another opportunity to find this many people who knew Elody in one place," I suggested.

Juliet and I moved into the crowd and eavesdropped on the surrounding conversations. Jay Burns walked onto the stage and launched into a rambling tribute about Elody and their love.

"Elody was my muse," Jay said and wiped a tear from his eye. "Her bright spirit and belief in my talent inspired me and launched my art career. Now she is gone, and I feel I can no longer paint with the same talent and emotion. I plan to finish my final few paintings as a tribute to her memory then retire my paintbrushes. You'll see me on the big screen instead as I commit myself fully to a career in acting."

Jay's announcement caused a furor of camera flashes and clicks as the reporters surged forward to pepper him with questions about his sudden decision. He held up his hands for silence. "This is a shock for the art world, but my heartbreak over the loss of my muse is too painful for me to continue. Tonight is about Elody. I'll release a statement to the press after the memorial service. Thank you."

"I'm surprised he would quit this early in his career especially since he found a style that worked for him and was successful," a woman standing next to us commented.

"Are you familiar with his artwork?" I asked her. She appeared how I imagined artists would. She wore a long skirt, large chunky jewelry and Birkenstocks, plus her fingers had paint stains on them.

"I was his art teacher before he dropped out of high school his junior year. I came here for the artist's retreat. Imagine my surprise to see a former student in Miller's Cove. I didn't realize he kept up with his art. He had no ambition as a teenager nor much talent," she informed us. "I don't mean to sound unkind, but his main talent was copying other students' styles. He never had an art style of his own."

"Maybe Elody was his muse and helped him tap into his talent," Juliet offered. "I'm Juliet Jefferson. I'll be down at the community center tomorrow morning teaching a yoga class for the artist's retreat if you'd care to join me."

"Pam Guynn. Sounds relaxing and I love yoga. I hope I didn't sound too negative. It's not that I begrudge Jay his success. I'm just puzzled by how well he's developed his own style after what I saw in the past," Pam said.

"Puzzling indeed," Juliet bobbed her head in agreement. "We'd better head for home before it gets too late. Yoga's at six sharp. I'll see you there."

We walked to the park exit and headed for my house. I mulled over everything I learned today. The Senator was off the suspect list. Jay attributed his talent and success directly to Elody. Why would he kill the figurative cash cow? With Elody gone, he claimed he could no longer paint. Tessa had nothing but disdain for Elody, but did that translate into murder? I wasn't sure. My suspects weren't looking too guilty at this point. I hoped I discovered more when I met with Elody's father Monday evening for dinner.

"Ah, crud biscuits!" I exclaimed.

"That was random. What's up?"

"I'm meeting Senator Campbell for dinner tomorrow night, but I'm supposed to have dinner with Clint and his new partner tomorrow night," I explained.

"You couldn't turn down dinner with a state senator who wants to speak to you about his daughter," Juliet said.

"True. I'll reschedule my dinner with Clint and Lu. He'll be fine with it."

"Of course he will," Juliet murmured.

"What?" I asked surprised at the negative tone in Juliet's voice.

"It's nothing. It seems to me that Clint isn't as invested in the relationship as you are. He doesn't care enough to get upset. Just ignore me. I'm probably wrong," Juliet said with an apologetic grin.

"Clint cares," I protested. "He's reserved, but he's always been that way. It's his personality."

"I'm sorry. I shouldn't have said anything. Pick you up at five thirty. *Ciao!*" Juliet climbed into Ole Blue and left.

I thought about what she said. Clint came across as reserved, but it was how his aunt raised him. My family was demonstrative, but that didn't mean every family was. He spent time at our house growing up because he lived with his great aunt. She didn't care for rambunctious teens running around her home. He never talked about his parents and his life before he came to Miller's Cove. I never asked because I figured talking about their death was too painful for him. Juliet was right. Clint did hold back too much about himself. I was an open, romantic fiction book, but he was a rare, archival tome locked tightly away in a vault. I wasn't a huge fan of rocking a boat that floated peacefully down the relationship river, but I should ask where he saw our relationship heading; however, that was a conversation for another day.

I called Clint to tell him good night, but it went straight to voicemail. "Howdy, lawman. This here is yer little lady. Got some bad news. We need to reschedule tomorrow night's dinner with Lu. Senator Campbell wants to talk to me at six tomorrow evening, so can we cook out on Tuesday? I promised Juliet I would go to butt crack o' dawn yoga, so I'm going to bed. I'll call you tomorrow." I stifled a yawn as I plugged my cell phone in to charge. All the excitement of the past two days, hauling boxes of books, and crime busting had exhausted me. I slipped on a pale blue cotton nightgown, brushed my teeth and climbed into bed. I heard Watson's little nails click across the floor as he settled down to sleep on his blanket next to my bed. I drifted off to sleep and didn't dream of dead girls at all.

CHAPTER SIXTEEN

Five o'clock came much too early. My alarm let out an incessant buzz until my hand crashed down on it. It fell off the nightstand with a loud crash. This caused Watson to yelp and Ferdie to claw her way across my legs. Ugh! Whose bright idea was it to do early morning yoga? Mine. Well, Juliet's idea if truth be told. I dragged my exhausted carcass to the shower and leaned against the shower wall until the warm jets of water became lukewarm.

Slightly more awake, I toweled off and dug out the one pair of yoga pants I owned. Juliet gave them to me last year for Christmas. They still had tags on them. I squeezed into them. Juliet must have forgotten my short curves required a slightly looser size than her slim, athletic frame. I pulled a long t-shirt over my damp curls so it could cover my ample rear. I walked into the kitchen and plugged in my percolator to start my coffee. Watson and I went out into my small backyard for his morning sniff and potty. His boundless terrier energy before the birds were even singing made me tired all over again.

Once he finished his daily doggie duties, I poured a cup of coffee and waited for Juliet. I contemplated double fisting the coffee so I wouldn't have to get up for a refill. I was halfway through my second cup when Juliet opened the kitchen door, stuck her head in and trilled, "Good morning, Merry Sunshine!"

If my glower didn't scare her, I doubted throwing my coffee cup at her head would phase her. Groaning, I hoisted myself out of the kitchen chair and trudged to her convertible. "I don't know how you do classes this early," I grumbled.

"It invigorates me. Once I work through my poses, I have energy for the rest of the day. Trust me. After this morning, you'll be begging to join my six a.m. class every day," Juliet said. She sipped on a straw stuck in a bottle of gelatinous green goo.

"What in the blue blazes are you drinking?" I gagged as she slurped the slimy mixture again.

"It is a spinach, banana, avocado and wheat grass smoothie. Great for the complexion, and it helps maximize my energy," Juliet slurped down another slug of slime and smiled at me. Her front teeth had a glob of green stuck between them. I didn't tell her. Paybacks for the early morning perkiness she refused to tone down to a more pleasant and tolerable level.

We pulled into the community center next to the lakeshore. Several yoga-panted women made their way into the center ahead of us. I spotted Willow in the group wearing a tie-dyed shirt and her dreads tied on top of her head. Juliet bounded behind them. I plodded after her and took my place at the back of the room.

A chubby girl rushed in right before class started. With stringy leaf-brown hair, glasses and grubby black velour sweatpants, she didn't seem like the type to enjoy yoga. Heck. Who was I kidding? I wasn't the type to enjoy yoga.

"Hi. I'm Phee. I'm new to yoga. How about you?" I whispered as Juliet encouraged us to breathe in through our noses and "ha" out our mouths.

"Shawna," she whispered back and lifted her arms as she inhaled. "Just follow the teacher the best you can. Yoga is about flow and energy. Don't push yourself past your comfort level." Shawna moved with a litheness that belied her bulky frame. "I've practiced yoga for years, but when I started, I was clumsier than a newborn calf."

I tried to follow Juliet as she progressed to something called a sun salutation. I couldn't keep up because I tried to watch the people attending the class with one eye and follow Juliet's movements with my other eye. As she instructed us to move into downward facing dog, I lifted my rear and heard a ripping noise. I felt a draft of cool air on my ample derriere. Holy toddlers in tiaras! My new yoga pants had split. I attempted to stand from my downward position, lost my balance and tumbled into the gray-haired woman to my right. This set in motion a domino effect as she crashed into the anemic girl next to her. As we fell into a jumbled mess of arms and legs, the rest of the class stopped and watched aghast at the chaos in the midst of their peaceful asana. I untangled myself and looked up to find Juliet glaring down at me.

Twenty minutes later and properly chastened, I wore a pair of Juliet's bike shorts which turned into capris on my short legs. I watched the class finish the last of their poses and bow with hands together and say, "Namaste."

"You weren't kidding when you said you were new," Shawna plopped down on the bench next to me. "I almost felt sorry for you. I thought the instructor would blow a gasket."

"She's my little sister. She has to be nice to me," I commented.

"Huh. You don't look like her at all." Shawna squinted as she examined me through her smudged lenses.

"No, I don't." Too tired and embarrassed to try to be polite, I asked, "Are you here for the artist's retreat?"

"Kind of. I came with my friend. Her family has a place here, but she didn't want to stay at their cabin. She'd had a falling out with her dad, so I rented a place for us on the far side of the lake. She is…was an artist," Shawna corrected herself.

"Are you talking about Elody Campbell?" I perked up as I realized this mousy girl might be a great source of information.

"Yeah. She and I were roommates in college before she dropped out."

"Really?" I must have looked incredulous because Shawna scowled at me.

"Yes, really. She wasn't like the press portrayed her at all. She didn't party and act crazy until her mom died. When she and I roomed together, Elody lived for her art. It was her plan to have her paintings hang in every major gallery in the country by her thirtieth birthday. When her mom died, she lost her drive and her painting changed. She stopped caring about anything. She'd paint and then toss the finished canvases in the trash. After a few months, she packed her bags and left before the semester was over," Shawna said.

"Elody was a good painter?" I asked. It was more of a statement than a question. Nicolette had said Elody's paintings were exceptional. I wondered why Jay, not Elody, caught the art world's eye if she possessed so much talent.

"Her art was amazing." Shawna said with the fervor of a true fan. "I'm a microbiologist. Correction. I'm a PhD candidate in microbiology. I'm not in the cool, art crowd like the rest of these people, but Elody's talent knocked a nerd like me off my feet."

"Wow! I'd like to see some of her work." I hoped Shawna had access to some of Elody's paintings.

"So would I," Shawna gave a rueful shake of her head. "Someone broke into our cabin yesterday. The only things stolen were Elody's paintings. They even stole her unfinished pieces."

"How horrible!" I exclaimed. Elody's death seemed inextricably entwined with art. Who would steal the paintings of a talented, but undiscovered artist? Could an obsessed fan have taken them when they learned of Elody's murder? Instead of yoga clearing my head, it felt muddled by my latest discovery.

CHAPTER SEVENTEEN

I chatted with Shawna for a few more minutes about her work in microbiology. She seemed lost and lonely amongst the artistic crowd, so I invited her to meet me for lunch tomorrow at the Quickie Cow. I wanted to ask her some additional questions about Elody, but didn't want to arouse her suspicions about my motives. Natural curiosity was normal, but a more than casual curiosity about crime made people uneasy.

I walked outside to wait for Juliet. I didn't want to face the other women after my earlier fiasco. Pulling a paperback out of my purse, I sat down on one of the bright purple Adirondack chairs by the lake shore. A few minutes later, I was immersed in the latest Thyme for Tea cozy mystery. Just as the heroine discovered a dead body in her hall closet, a shadow fell across my page. Annoyed at the unexpected interruption, I squinted up at my cozy crime interloper. Jay Burns stood over me. I squelched my annoyance and seized the opportunity to learn more about Jay and Elody's relationship.

"Hello," I gave him a friendly smile.

"Hey there. Whatcha reading?" Jay squatted down next to me. He plucked a small wildflower from the patch in front of him.

"*Just in Thyme for Death.*" I showed him the cover of the book in my hand. "It's a murder mystery." Pickles and pancakes! Someone killed his girlfriend and here I am showing him a murder mystery. I fidgeted with the hem of my shirt and wondered how to bring up Elody.

"You like to read? Me? Not so much. I'd rather work with my hands. I'm Jay, by the way." He held out the small white flower. As he leaned forward to hand it to me, a lock of his dark hair escaped from his short ponytail and fell across his cheek. Up close, I could see his appeal. He still had a grungy air about him, but his dark eyes and olive complexion gave him a pirate-like sex appeal. The tattoos on his arms added to his roguish appearance. He smelled of sandalwood and patchouli.

I took the flower from him and sniffed it. "I'm Phee. So what brings you here? Are you waiting for someone in the yoga class?"

"Nah. I couldn't sleep. I got tired of staring at the walls of my room. Figured I'd take a walk. So what's a beautiful girl doing reading a book down by the lake in the early morning hours? I'm surprised your husband isn't serving you breakfast in bed," Jay winked and the corner of his mouth curved up in a half smile.

"I'm not married." I blushed as the thought of Jay bringing me breakfast in bed flitted through my mind. What was wrong with me? I must have bumped my head when I fell. "I'm waiting for my sister. She taught the yoga class this morning."

"Yoga, huh? Never tried it. Mind if I keep you company for a few minutes?" Jay eased the rest of the way down and stretched his legs out on the grass. He leaned back and gave me a bold once-over. He had the tightly coiled energy of a jaguar waiting to pounce on its prey. I sensed danger despite his warm smile.

"No one waiting to bring you breakfast?" I asked, not meeting his gaze.

He leaned back on his arms and let the sun warm his face. He didn't respond right away. "No. My girlfriend's gone."

Seizing the moment, I probed further. "You broke up with her? Is that why you couldn't sleep?"

Jay lowered his head. "My girlfriend was Elody Campbell. Someone killed her."

"I'm so sorry. I didn't realize…" I acted like I was at a loss for words. I certainly couldn't ask him if he killed her.

"It's okay. I'm still coming to terms with it. Bad thing is we had a big fight a few weeks ago. Now I'll never know if we could've worked it out."

"I understand. Closure is important," I nodded sagely. "Can I be nosy and ask why you fought?"

"Ah, that's the million dollar question. I guess you could say I'm between two worlds. We all do stupid things we regret later," Jay said. He stood up and brushed the dry grass off his jeans. "It's too nice of a morning to sit here and talk about mistakes and murder with a beautiful woman. I'll leave you to your book. I've got business to take care of anyway. It was nice to meet you, Phee. I hope to see you again soon." He gave me a two-finger salute and strolled off leaving me wondering if I met a heartbroken hottie or a contrite killer.

The door to the community center opened and a group of women spilled out laughing and chattering. Juliet peeled away and waved goodbye to them. I stood up and trotted to Ole Blue. Her glare warned me not to joke about my downward dog disaster. She stalked past me and threw her yoga mat in the backseat. I followed meekly behind her and climbed into the passenger seat without a word.

"Don't speak. You fell over and took out two people!" Juliet exclaimed.

"But I…" I protested, but she raised her hand up to stop me.

"I told you yoga wasn't easy, but no, you didn't listen to me. To make up for causing me trauma and years of therapy, you'll wake up and attend my early morning yoga class for the next year. For pity's sake, learn how to at least do a sun salutation."

"Okay." I bit my lip. I would be happy to get up at the crack of dawn to make it up to her. "I'm sorry if I embarrassed you with my little slip and fall."

"Oh, it was a little more than a slip and fall. You body-slammed the artist, Alicia Staunton. She's won every major art critic's heart in the state with her latest show. Thank the goddess, you didn't break her hand or worse. I'd never be able to show my face at the ashram again." Juliet continued to scowl as she steered Ole Blue out of the parking lot.

"I promise to practice every single day. I'll never do downward facing dog again without a safety net." I raised my right hand to swear.

"That's the smartest thing you've done all day," Juliet said. Her face lost some of the angry tightness. "You weebled and wobbled, then you fell down!" Her face split into a wide grin.

"I can never show my face there again," I relaxed as the tension eased.

"I wouldn't worry too much about it. On the up side, I found out an interesting tidbit of information," Juliet said.

"Me, too. You go first," I offered as a gesture of peacemaking penitence.

"One of the women confided that Elody argued with her friend the night before she died. It's the girl you didn't take out with your downward dog debacle. The one with the glasses and brown hair."

"Shawna Collins. I talked to her after class. She roomed with Elody in college. She's not your typical club kid or groupie Elody partied with. Shawna is smart and a doctoral candidate in microbiology."

"I don't even know what a microbiologist studies. According to Rachel Mick, whose cabin is next to Elody's, she and Shawna had a knock-down, drag-out screaming match. Rachel wasn't sure what the fight was about, but she heard Shawna yell at Elody that she was acting stupid, and if Elody didn't do something about it, she would," Juliet said.

"I'm surprised. Shawna sounded like she adored Elody. If what Rachel told you is the truth, then maybe Shawna took care of things by taking out Elody," I concluded.

CHAPTER EIGHTEEN

I pondered what I learned about Shawna as Juliet cruised along the road that hugged the lakeshore. She didn't seem like a murdering madwoman, but then does anyone ever look like the killers you see in the movies? "I'm having lunch with Shawna tomorrow. I'll try to find out what she and Elody were arguing about that night. I had an interesting run-in with someone myself."

"Glad you did something productive this morning to make up for your lack of coordination," Juliet joked. She kept her eyes trained on the road ahead and concentrated on the non-existent traffic, but I caught the quick smirk and side glance.

"My mind is a ninja master of coordination. My body just hasn't caught up yet. So do you want to hear who I talked to, or would you like to mock me a few minutes more?"

"Oh, I can hold my mocking to a minimum for at least ten minutes. Spill it, Ninja Librarian," Juliet demanded. She turned into my driveway and parked her car.

"Jay Burns. He's better looking in person. He's like a rebel without a clue. He caught me by surprise when he walked up to me, so I wasn't able to probe too much into his relationship with Elody. Jay didn't seem heartbroken when I talked to him, but maybe he's pulled himself together since yesterday. According to him, he and Elody had a big fight, and they'd split," I said.

"Did he tell you what they fought about?" Juliet asked.

"Not really. He said something about being torn between two worlds. Maybe Elody wanted back into her dad's good graces, and an older street thug turned artist didn't cut it in the Senator's high profile, political world," I offered. "I didn't tell him I was your sister, so play dumb and pretend you forgot to tell me he was joining us for lunch."

"It will be a stretch to play clueless, but I'll persevere." Juliet laid the back of her hand against her forehead and sighed. Such a comedy queen. She should have been on stage rather than a yoga mat.

"Thank you for sacrificing yourself on my behalf." I rolled my eyes as I opened the car door. "I better hustle. Today's the start of summer reading. I told Wade we needed to get to work early to get the bags ready to hand out to the children. I'll meet you in front of the restaurant at one, okay?"

"Sounds good. Later days and crazy ways, chick." Juliet waved and backed out of the driveway. I raised my hand and waved back as she zipped away in her convertible.

The paper boy had missed my front porch again. I spotted the *Miller's Cove Courier* resting atop my hedges. I grabbed it on my way inside and tossed it on the hallway table. After loving on Watson and Ferdie a few minutes, I hurried and changed my clothes.

A half an hour later, I walked into work and saw Wade had beaten me there. Webster's Dictionary defined punctuality with a picture of Wade. As his boss, I couldn't complain. As his friend, I was glad he accepted Juliet's chronic ignorance of time when it came to anything but yoga.

"Your girlfriend is a mini-dictator," I said in the way of greeting. "I went to her six a.m. yoga class. You have one little mishap where you land on a few famous artists and she can't ignore it and let it go." I put my purse into my desk drawer and turned to complain about Juliet's lack of compassion for my traumatic event.

"Huh. That's nice," Wade responded. He didn't bother to glance up. He continued flipping through the mail.

I sensed something wasn't right in Wade World, so I leaned against the counter and said, "Yeah. She said from now on she was teaching all of her yoga classes in the nude. It's all the rage in New York City."

"That's cool," Wade said and turned to check in the books sitting on the book cart.

I reached over and rolled the cart out of his reach. "What's up with you? Don't you dare say nothing because I'll know you're lying."

Instead of responding, he handed me the *Miller's Cove Courier.* The headline read "Senator Campbell Holds Memorial Service for Murdered Daughter." Puzzled, I said, "Juliet and I went to the service last night. Remember?"

"Open it and check out page two," Wade yanked the cart back towards him and grabbed two books to scan.

I set the paper on the counter and flipped to page two. Photographs of the Senator and several small-time celebrities attending the service filled the page. Halfway down, there was a picture of Juliet leaning in close to talk to Jay. The caption read, "No moss grows on Jay Burns as he nuzzles his newest love interest less than twenty-four hours after girlfriend Elody's tragic murder." Crap on a cracker. No wonder Wade seemed angry. Thank goodness they hadn't used Juliet's name. The paparazzi were such scavengers. How could they take an innocent moment and turn it into a sordid affair? I scanned the rest of the pictures. In the bottom left corner, a picture showed Jay watching Juliet walk away from him. He ogled her departing derriere. I felt greasy and dirty just looking at his expression. The earlier caption was correct. He didn't appear lovelorn over Elody's death.

"You realize she and I were on the job," I explained to Wade. He continued to ignore me and studied the children's book in his hand like it was an American classic with profound wisdom in its pages. "We were investigating Elody's murder. I assigned Juliet to corner Jay. It was loud, and cameras were everywhere. She leaned in to tell him what time to meet us today for lunch. The camera jockey snapped pictures and twisted it to sell papers. My sister thinks you're the hottest thing since siracha peanuts went on sale at Abe's. Jay Burns is a C-minus aspiring to reach your A-plus magnificence."

Wade tried to stay silent, but a second later he cracked a smile. "Where do you come up with these things? I'll take that A-plus magnificence and own it. I would like that exact wording on my next evaluation, please."

"You got it. It was crazy last night. It was more of a red carpet photo op than memorial for Elody. Cameras and reporters packed the park, and half the town showed up to watch the drama unfold."

"I'm sorry I missed the chaos. I'm also sorry I came across like a caveman guarding his mastodon meat. What kind of man would I be if I didn't get jealous when that loser 'artiste' looked like he wanted to have his way with my woman? I love your sister, and I have a jealous streak. It's the nature of this A-plus magnificent man," Wade puffed out his chest and winked at me.

"You're killing me with your manliness," I laughed. "I understand completely. I wouldn't like it if the situation reversed and Clint appeared in the paper with another woman."

I grabbed the box of bags and began to stuff them with reading logs and t-shirts for the children. Wade stood up and rolled the cart around to the front of the desk. "I'm glad you understand. Clint would shoot this Jay Burns creep if he was in my shoes. I showed remarkable restraint."

Wade continued towards the stacks to shelve the books. I paused in my bag stuffing and thought about what Wade said. Would Clint be jealous or would he shrug it off? Was he invested in me as much as I was in him? Shrugging off my doubts, I hurried to finish so I could open the library and kick off summer reading fun.

CHAPTER NINETEEN

At nine o' clock, I unlocked the door and prepared for the onslaught of excited summer readers. Several moms stood outside with their children. When I opened the door, I stepped back to avoid being trampled by an antsy toddler dashing towards the reading tent set up for the summer. I spent most of the morning darting between the circulation desk to hand out bags and the children's area to help pick out books.

"My Jordan is an exceptionally bright child," Missy Kirkland informed me. "I want him to read chapter books this summer."

"There's a great series for beginning chapter readers over here," I said and guided her towards the Pete the Pirate series popular with second grade readers. Jordan wandered away from his mother and picked up a picture book about whales.

"Jordan, come here!" Missy demanded. She snapped her fingers and pointed to the shelves next to her. "You're going to read big boy books this summer."

Jordan scowled and threw the picture book on the floor. He crossed his arms and stomped over to where his mother sorted through Pete the Pirate books. I picked up the whale book and took it to the desk with me. I would persuade Missy to transition Jordan to chapter books by reading one picture book a week along with the "bigger boy books." Helicopter moms, determined their child would be the next genius bound for Harvard, took the joy out of reading. They insisted on pushing higher level books on their kids before they were ready. As a librarian, I wanted to make sure kids liked to read, so they would become lifetime book lovers.

"Miss Phee! Miss Phee!" I heard a little voice calling for me. I searched the children's area and spotted eight-year-old Ainsley sitting on the floor surrounded by a stack of books.

I sat on the floor next to her crisscrossing my feet under my knees. "How are you, Ainsley? I haven't seen you for three weeks. I've missed my best reader," I said. Ainsley came every few days and walked out with a stack of books almost as tall as she was.

"I visited my grandma. She had no good books at her house, and she made me play outside all day. It sucked!" Ainsley complained. "I can't remember which Nancy Drew I read last." She peered down at two of the books she held in her hands.

"If I remember correctly, it was *The Clue of the Tapping Heels.* You decided you wanted a Persian kitten after reading it. We talked about how hard Persians were to brush and keep clean," I said. I picked up *The Mystery of the Brass-bound Trunk* and handed it to her. "This is the next book in the series. You'll like it. Nancy goes on a trip and her trunk gets mixed up with someone else's. Smugglers, stolen jewelry and dark warnings. It's all very mysterious."

"Thanks. I don't mind reading a book again, but there are only so many days in summer break. I plan to read every one of the Nancy Drew books before school starts."

I helped her pick up her stack of books. I checked them out and told her I'd see her in a few days. Glancing at the clock, I realized it was almost one. Claire had come in at noon to help, so I could safely leave the library for a little while. I told Wade I was meeting Juliet for lunch and would bring him back a sandwich and chips.

"You make sure Jay Burns knows I have his number and I'm not afraid to dial it." Wade cracked his knuckles and flexed his muscles.

"Good golly. Settle down, Muscles Malone. You've been reading the true crime mafia books again, haven't you?" I picked up my purse and left for Odd Couple's.

It was wall-to-wall diners when I arrived a few minutes later. Seth sprinted between tables as Stephanie worked the register. Zachary Towson, a high school student and star soccer player, nearly mowed me down as he carried a bus pan to the back.

"Sorry, Miss Jefferson. It's crazy busy in here. All the reporters and stuff showed up for lunch. Are you looking for your sister? She's in the back corner booth by the restrooms," Zach said and then scurried through the swinging doors to the kitchen.

Juliet waved at me, and I worked my way to her booth. Jay sat across from her. He raised his eyebrows when he saw me sit down next to Juliet. Seth walked past on his way to the back and took my drink order.

"This is my sister, Phee. Phee, Jay Burns," Juliet introduced us.

"Juliet, you didn't tell me Jay was joining us for lunch. He and I met this morning while I waited for you to finish teaching class." I twirled one of my stray curls around my finger. "It's nice to see you again."

"I didn't realize Juliet was your sister. Aren't I the lucky guy eating lunch with two gorgeous women?" Jay gave me a predatory once over that reminded me of the wolf in Little Red Riding Hood. The photo in the paper of him ogling Juliet made me view him with a wary eye.

"You're too kind," I said. I sensed rather than saw the reporters in the restaurant waiting to pounce. It wouldn't surprise me if they snapped pictures of us with their cell phones from underneath their tables to sell to the tabloids.

"You must be overwhelmed by all these ghouls invading your privacy and not allowing you to grieve for Elody." I gave him my best sympathetic smile.

"You've no idea how hard it is," Jay agreed as he hung his head and heaved a deep sigh. "They hound me day and night. I've been keeping my chin up and my head low to try to get through the horror of all of this." He waved his hands at the room. A few diners stared at us openly over the tops of their menus. Reporters thinking they were on covert operations.

"You're a trooper. I couldn't do it. I'd be an emotional wreck," Juliet sympathized. "I heard Elody was here in Miller's Cove for the women's art retreat. Did you get a chance to see her before she died?"

Juliet's boldness didn't surprise me. I may channel Nancy Drew and Miss Marple when talking to suspects, but Juliet was straight Pepper Anderson with a little Cagney and

Lacey tossed into the personality mix. All the cop shows she watched the past year were coming in handy. I should watch them myself to get some pointers.

"I hadn't seen her in about a month. It's like I told your sister this morning, we argued and Elody packed her things and left."

"How sad for you?" Juliet leaned forward and did her best imitation of my mother's concerned face. The girl had mad acting skills. "Was it an awful fight? I've been through some rocky relationships. It's hard when you argue and don't make up afterward. Feelings fester and sometimes you never get to say how you feel."

My jaw dropped in awe of Juliet's subtle digging at the truth. I took a quick gulp of my root beer to hide my astonishment. Seth headed towards our table, but I gave him a furtive shake of my head. He nodded his understanding and pivoted on his heels towards the table nearby to hand them their check.

Jay leaned forward and lowered his voice. "Elody and I fought over art. She wanted me to help her get her paintings into a few galleries. She got angry when I told her she needed to work on her technique before she tried to sell any pieces. I explained to her how vicious critics could be towards new artists. She wouldn't listen and said I didn't support her need to express herself through her art." His eyes darted around the room as he spoke to us.

"Did she have any talent, or was she hoping your name would help her become famous?" I asked. "That sounded rude, didn't it? I'm sorry. I assume you get people trying to make money off of you or use your connections in the art world. Elody had her own connections through her family, didn't she?"

"She used to, but since she and her dad parted company, his old cronies wouldn't take her calls," Jay confided. "Her paintings weren't too bad. They lacked personality, and her style imitated too many other artists."

"You tried to protect her feelings because you cared about her," Juliet offered.

"Exactly. Now I would give anything to hang her paintings next to mine in a gallery. Too bad she destroyed all her art when she left me." Jay scratched at his neck and sighed. I wondered how much of this was real and how much was him playing the role of grieving lover. After all, he had announced his plan to pursue acting as a career.

A hand came to rest on my shoulder. I glanced up and saw Clint. My heart flip-flopped. I slid out of the booth and hugged him. "When did you get back? You didn't call me. Did you get my message about tonight? I missed you!" I stood on my tiptoes and gave him a quick kiss.

"Whoa. Slow down and take a breath. I got back about twenty minutes ago. Wade told me you were here, so I decided to try to have lunch with my favorite girlfriend. I don't want to interrupt, so I can wait and see you after work," Clint said as he eyed Jay's pierced ears and tattoos.

"This is Jay Burns, Elody Campbell's boyfriend," I said. "Jay, Clint Mason. You'll probably need to talk to him about Elody and the investigation. He's a deputy sheriff."

Jay stood up and held out his hand. "Nice to meet you. I hate to cut things short, but all this talk about Elody has made me lose my appetite. Can I get a rain check?" He pulled out a fifty dollar bill and threw it on the table.

"Uh, sure. I didn't mean to upset you," Juliet said. "You don't need to pay for lunch though."

"It's okay. I've got a meeting over at Stone Street Gallery this afternoon. Allow me the pleasure of buying the two prettiest girls in town lunch. Deputy, nice meeting you." Jay maneuvered through the crowded diner and out the front door. A few people stood up and sprinted after him with cameras in hand.

"Who knew my presence could clear a room," Clint joked as he eased into Jay's vacated spot. "What I want to know is what you two are doing eating lunch with a suspect?"

"Jay's a suspect?" Juliet gave Clint a wide-eyed innocent look. "I ran into him at the memorial service. We talked, and I invited him to eat lunch with us. It sounds like the police have made progress in the case if you're naming suspects."

"Cut the innocent act, Juls. You and Phee look as guilty as my cat when he knocks all the knick-knacks off the shelf," Clint said. "I'm gone less than a week, and the whole town is turned upside-down. Let me rephrase my earlier comment. Jay is a person of interest in an ongoing investigation. Satisfied?"

"Sheesh. Rain on my interrogation parade, why don't you?" Juliet shot back. Her look said she dared him to give her grief over investigating. "For your information, we found out he argued with Elody over her desire to pursue art as a career."

"But he lied," I blurted out. "I talked to her roommate, Shawna, and to Nicolette Simon. Both women said Elody possessed real talent. Why would she need Jay's help to get discovered? Either they lied, or Jay did. My money is on Jay. He's lying like a hound dog on a hearth rug." I nodded my head in satisfaction as I mentally moved Jay to the top of my suspect list.

CHAPTER TWENTY

Seth came and took our order. We decided to share Buddy Holly Baked Nachos with extra guacamole for Juliet and me. Clint wrinkled his nose when Juliet added it to our order.

"What? Avocados are good for you," Juliet protested.

"It looks like the inside of the twins' diapers. I can't do it. You keep your green goo away from my chips, woman, or I won't be responsible for my actions," Clint warned.

I moved around the booth to sit next to him. He gave my thigh a quick squeeze under the table and I leaned against him.

"Watson lived up to his name. He's the one who discovered Elody's body. You should be upset with him for dragging me into this mess," I said.

"He likes finding dead things, but it's usually just a field mouse or one of my stinky socks," Clint said. "The sheriff gave me an update over the phone. We didn't release the information about the killer's stabbing the paintbrush into her chest. You need to keep it under wraps."

"We are. I took a picture of the crime scene with my phone. Let me show you," I said. I pulled my phone from my purse and showed him the few photos I'd taken.

"Ew. You didn't tell me you took pictures. Even I'm not that hardened of an investigator," Juliet said. Her nose scrunched, and she gagged.

"I didn't take a picture of her body, silly goose. I took a picture of the canvas next to her. It looked like she tried to leave a clue. She tried to write the name of the killer," I told her. "I can't decipher what letter or word she tried to write because of the smeared paint. It doesn't help us out much."

"The problem with your theory is she may not have written a name of a person, but a place," Clint said. He handed the phone to Juliet so she could view the pictures.

"You're right. It could be anyone or anywhere. Did the sheriff tell you that Elody took paintings to Stone Street Gallery to sell on commission?" I mulled this over, then added, "I think we need to dig into Nic's background a little more. She's only lived in Miller's Cover for two years. What do we really know about her?"

"I thought that after last year you'd stay away from murder investigations. I might need to lock you in a closet and flick Fruity Loops under the door to feed you and keep you safe," Clint threatened. He wrapped his arm around my shoulder and pulled me closer.

"I'll take Juliet with me. It's not like I can avoid Nic anyway. We volunteer at the summer camp together. I'll stop by the gallery on my way back to work. I can be subtle. As a matter of fact, Mom thought about naming me Subtlety, but Dad overrode her. As much as I appreciate your manly protection, you can't wrap me in cotton and lock me in a box," I said and pulled away from him a little. "I do like Fruity Loops though."

"I get it." Clint held his hands up in surrender. "I'll knock off the overprotective attitude if you'll promise to be careful. This person already killed once. There's no guarantee they won't do it again. The same goes for you, Juliet. I'd never forgive myself if anything happened to either of you."

"Ooh, Clint. I love it when you get all big brother protective with me. If you lock me in the closet with Phee, flick me Oat Rings instead," Juliet joked. "All kidding aside, Phee, he's right. I don't want a repeat of last year. Safety first is my new motto!" Juliet raised her right hand in the three-fingered scout promise.

"Glad you see the wisdom of my ways," Clint said dryly. "Phee, what time is your dinner with Senator Campbell? If you don't get back too late, I'll come by your house."

"It's at six. I'm sorry I had to cancel our dinner this evening, but how do you say no to a senator? He wanted to hear from me what I found rather than accept what he called the "sanitized report" he received from Sheriff Dawes. I haven't a clue what I can add."

"He wasn't told about the postmortem stabbing, only the gunshot wound. He also doesn't know about the clue left on the canvas. You'll have to give him a sanitized report yourself," Clint advised.

Juliet leaned forward and scooped guacamole onto a chip. "Does Sheriff Dawes suspect Senator Campbell of being involved in the murder?"

"Not at all. We haven't ruled out his staff though. His closest staff member is a guy named Anthony Ziegfried. From our preliminary background check, he is a mover and a shaker in the political world. He plans to ride someone's coattails to the White House. Who knows what he would do to make sure Elody didn't hurt Senator Campbell's chances." Clint refused to look at Juliet and me as we crunched our guacamole-smeared chips. He shuddered when his eyes fell on the bowl as he reached for a glob of cheesy beef-laden chips.

"Anthony is a sweetheart," I said. "He's very charming. He'll be at the dinner tonight, I'm sure. I can't believe he would commit murder for a political campaign."

"Just don't be fooled by any of these political types. They make their bread and butter by smooth talk and polished good looks," Clint warned.

"Mrs. Lassiter has known Senator Campbell since he was a child. She went to college with the Senator's mother," I said. "By the way, I learned what happened to Mr. Lassiter yesterday. It turns out he died their first year of marriage. She never remarried because he was her one true love." I sighed. It was so romantic to pine for your one true love. I could relate.

"Sounds foolish. No one should base their whole existence on another person. It's not healthy," Clint said matter-of-factly. He took a sip of his iced tea.

"Mrs. Lassiter didn't base her whole existence on her husband," I argued. "She felt that no one else could ever live up to the love she had with George. I don't care what you say. It's sad and romantic." I made a point of waving a chip weighed down with guacamole under his nose.

"It sounds like one of you classic movie plots you love so much. I live in the real world, so I guess I'm just a practical guy." Clint leaned back and rubbed his stomach with both hands. "I'm stuffed. It's almost two, and I told the sheriff I would stop back by the office before going home and unpacking my bag. I'll pick up Watson on my way home. Is his food in the cupboard by the sink?"

"Yes," I grumbled and refused to meet his eyes.

"Call me later." He leaned in for a kiss goodbye. I gave him a quick peck and slid out of the booth so he could leave. I smiled a tight smile that didn't reach my eyes, then sat back down.

"I will," I promised half-heartedly. After I watched him walk out, I turned to Juliet. "I'm mad at you!"

"At me? Why?"

"Before you made your little comments about Clint and his lack of commitment, I was happy and content. Now, I can't stop wondering if I'm fooling myself into thinking he and I might have a future. Maybe I'm still just living a schoolgirl fantasy. Or maybe, everything's just fine and you've made me paranoid." I scowled across the table at her. I stabbed my straw up and down in my glass to break up the ice in the bottom.

"Hold on, Phee. I gave you my honest opinion. Clint's held himself back since we were kids. He's the proverbial strong and silent type. His aunt was old-fashioned and reserved. I'm sure she raised him to control his emotions. What were his parents like? Maybe they weren't demonstrative either." Juliet said.

"Never asked. It's awkward bringing up his mom and dad. Their deaths must have been the most traumatic event in his life. When he's ready to tell me about them, he will.

I'm not like you, Juls. I don't feel comfortable poking at an open sore."

"You should talk to Mom," Juliet suggested. "She may have known Clint's parents when they were alive. They could have been stuffy like his aunt. If that's the case, as long as you're happy with him, my opinion shouldn't matter."

"I'll talk to Mom, but do me a favor. Don't fill my brain with any more doubts. My inner voice is a chatterbox all by itself. It doesn't need you to encourage it," I joked half-heartedly.

"Fair enough. I hope your inner voice talks to you about your yoga skills. It was asleep this morning when you went to my class." Juliet looked up at the ceiling and around the room whistling under her breath.

"Everyone's a comedian in my life. How did I get to be such a lucky gal?" I made a mental note to buy Juliet clown shoes to wear with her hot pink bedazzled mask.

CHAPTER TWENTY ONE

I bought Wade a sandwich and left Odd Couple's. As I walked down the street, I paused in front of Glimpse of the Past, an antique store specializing in vintage clothing. Miller's Cove was the hot spot in the state for antique hounds. Out of all the shops in the area, this one was my favorite. I peered in the store window to get a closer look at the cameo brooch pinned to a mannequin's lace-front blouse. As I leaned closer, I saw a reflection in the glass. I turned and spotted Clint deep in conversation with a short, blonde woman. It wasn't anyone I knew from town. He clearly knew her because he laughed at whatever she said. She playfully pushed him down the sidewalk. A slow, angry heat coursed through my body. No wonder he didn't get jealous or seem interested in moving our relationship forward. He had his next girlfriend already lined up. I wiped away a tear. *He's not worth crying over,* I thought. Straightening my shoulders and sniffling, I marched back to work.

I handed Wade his lunch. If he noticed my strained smile, he didn't comment. He took a paperback and went to the picnic table outside the back door to eat his lunch. I didn't have time to worry about Clint and his new lady love since our summer readers were out in full force today. The children loved the first day of the summer reading program as they set their goals and picked out new books to read. Each week throughout the summer, my volunteers and I had story hour, crafts, and Science Time with Sid. Sid was Mr. Sidnor, a retired high school science teacher who showed kids how to do experiments with everyday objects. It was by far our most popular program with the upper elementary and middle school crowd. I spent the afternoon speaking to parents about new books and the scheduled activities. By the time five o'clock arrived, I was dead on my feet.

When I arrived home, there was a small bouquet of Gerber daisies tied with a ribbon and a note attached. *Phee, It will be my pleasure to pick you up at 5:45 and drive you to our dinner with Senator Campbell. – Anthony Ziegfried.* I smiled at the thoughtfulness and unlocked the front door to make a mad dash for the shower. I had twenty minutes before Anthony arrived. I planned to be a sophisticated socialite rather than a frumpy bookworm.

I chose a light blue sundress with small pink flowers embroidered around the hem of the skirt. Pearl stud earrings with a matching choker-style necklace contrasted nicely with my light tan. I twisted my red curls into a quick chignon and pulled a few curls loose to frame my face. A hint of blush and mascara, then I was ready to go.

I heard a knock on my front door. Anthony stood on my porch in a navy blue polo shirt and khakis. "Would you like to come in for a minute?" I offered.

"Just for a minute. The Senator is a stickler for punctuality." Anthony stepped into the hallway and looked around. I had a large art deco mirror hanging above a demi lune table. A small Tiffany lamp sat on it. Anthony walked over and touched the shade. "Is this a real Tiffany lamp?"

"Yes. It belonged to my grandmother. I credit her with making me an antique hound. She left me several beautiful pieces. You're welcome to walk around if you'd like. I need to grab my purse, then I'll be ready to leave," I said. He wandered into my living room and perused my bookshelves. In my room, I dumped my large messenger bag out onto my bed. It didn't match the sophisticated ensemble I wore, so it needed to go. I found a small blue clutch in a drawer and put my wallet, cell phone and a lipstick in it. I smoothed my hair one last time in the mirror and spritzed perfume on my wrists and neck.

Anthony had found his way into my kitchen and gazed in wonder at my antique kitchen appliances. "I love your house. All the treasures you have tucked in here are amazing," he said.

"Thank you. I spend my free time digging through antique shops and flea markets for things to restore. Some people don't like antiques, but to me, they are gently-loved pieces of history looking for new homes," I said.

Anthony guided me out my front door to a dark sedan. As he drove out of town and towards the lake, I told him about growing up in Miller's Cove. "It sounds like an amazing place to raise a family. Good schools, peaceful town, low crime. This is the kind of town I'd like to move to once I start a family," Anthony said.

"Are you married?" I asked. I hadn't seen a wedding ring, but not everyone wore one.

"Not yet. I haven't found the right woman to put up with me. I might seem like an awesome catch, but looks can be deceiving. You aren't looking for a husband are you? I'm fairly fresh off the showroom floor, low miles, easy maintenance. The only downside is the long hours I work and the amount of travel involved."

I laughed. "No, I'm not in the market, but I'll keep you in mind."

"I hope you don't mind, but I did a little check into your background. You graduated top of your class. You've lived here in Miller's Cove and in Burlington while in college. Rumor has it you date a deputy sheriff. No criminal record or unseemly gambling habits. So in a nutshell, you're attractive, smart and somewhat single," Anthony summed up. He pulled the car up to a large cabin and turned the engine off. He turned and said, "I'm interested. I'm being a little bold, but my time here is short. You intrigue me, Phee Jefferson. There's something sweet and sexy about you."

"Um, I'm…um," I stuttered. I coughed and tried again. "I'm flattered and a little overwhelmed. I don't even know how to respond."

"Don't say anything right now. Just consider it an open invitation. We'd better get inside before the Senator sends up a flare." He stepped out of the car and walked around to open my door for me. He crooked his elbow to escort me inside. I hesitated for a moment, but then recalling the sight of Clint laughing with the blonde, I placed my hand on his arm and walked inside with him.

Richard Campbell waited on the back deck for us. Anthony excused himself and left me alone with the Senator. There was a glass and wrought iron table set for dinner. He stood looking out at the water smoking a cigar. "Ah, Ophelia. You're a beautiful sight for this old man's eyes."

"Senator, thank you for sending Anthony to fetch me. I'm not familiar with all the hidden lanes and drives here at the lake, so you saved me some confusion." I offered my hand, and he gave it a firm shake.

"Call me Richard. I'm a senator when the press is around. The rest of the time, I'm just an ordinary guy who puts his proverbial pants on one leg at a time," Richard boomed. "Let me put out my cigar, and we can sit down and chat. Nasty habit, but I limit myself to one in the evenings. My late wife couldn't stand the smell of them, so I used to sneak outside to enjoy them." He gave me a wink.

"My dad does the same thing," I said. "You have a beautiful view of the lake."

"Elody loved to sit out here and paint in the early morning hours. She said the peacefulness inspired her art." Richard stood silently and stared at some distant horizon. He shook himself out of his reverie and waved me towards the table. "Please sit. Anthony prepared us a dinner fit for a king this evening."

"Anthony acts as your chef?" I asked. "I thought he was your aide."

"He is," Richard said, "but he cooks for me when my staff has the night off. To be honest, if it wasn't for his cooking, I'd eat a hot dog and chips and wash it down with a cold beer. Never learned to cook and I'm too old to start."

He reached over and poured himself a glass of wine from the bottle chilling in a small bucket on the table. Tilting it over my glass, he lifted his eyebrow to await my okay. "A small glass would be nice," I said. "Senator, sorry, Richard, I've given it some thought and I don't think there is much more I can add to what Sheriff Dawes already reported."

Richard Campbell sat back in his chair. His hand tightened around the stem of the wineglass. I waited for it to snap under the pressure. "I want to know if you saw anything at the park that could help me prove that low-life scum Jay Burns killed my baby girl."

CHAPTER TWENTY TWO

I sat there stunned by the Senator's question. I revisited the crime scene in my mind. The only thing related to Jay Burns was the common tie of painting. "Sir, I saw her briefly before I realized she was dead then ran and called the police. Afterwards, they took over the scene. I'm not sure what I can add to what you already know," I stammered and plucked at a stray thread on the placemat in front of me.

"Hmm...the sheriff said the same thing. I'm having a difficult time processing that someone murdered my daughter. She was the joy of my life," Richard said. He reached into his back pocket and pulled out his wallet. Flipping it open, he held it out so I could see the photo of a little girl with silvery curls and a smile as wide as the ocean. She wore a pink ballet outfit and held the hand of what must have been the Senator in his younger years. "The only thing I have left of my family are my memories and photographs. No grandchildren. No one to carry on the Campbell name. My family's legacy ends with me and I want to catch the S.O.B. who ended it!" He snapped the wallet shut and tossed it on the table.

"I'm so sorry. I understand your grief and anger. If I knew anything, I swear I would tell you," I reassured him. "May I ask you a question about Elody?"

"Go ahead. If it helps catch her killer, I'll tell you anything you want to know." Richard leaned back and crossed his arms across his chest.

"Elody had been painting a landscape at the park. I found an unfinished picture with tubes of paint next to her. Did she do anything special or have any fancy brushes she preferred?"

"You're asking about a fancy brush because of the one found in her chest, aren't you?" He dropped his arms and leaned across the table to stare at me. The intensity of his gaze forced me to drop my eyes. Clint had said they had not disclosed that clue to anyone, but somehow Richard Campbell knew.

"I, uh…why do you say that?" I avoided his verbal trap.

"Young lady, I've learned to gain information in more ways than you can imagine. There is one person in every organization who has a gambling problem, owes back child support or has maxed out credit cards. Money goes a long way in greasing the rusty jaws of someone who is supposed to keep quiet," Richard said and gave a harsh bark of laughter. "I took less than five minutes to discover your entire life history. Oh, don't look at me like you're shocked. I had to make sure you weren't a criminal or the killer. Have no fear. You're cleaner than a frog's butt."

I gulped down my wine. I felt naked and exposed in front of this man I just met. Grief made people do strange things. This man in front of me dealt with his grief through action. If I was a parent, I imagined I'd do the same thing.

"It was a silver-handled paintbrush. It was old, possibly an antique. Did Elody paint with anything like that?" I asked. Since the cat was out of the bag, I didn't see the harm in discussing it.

"Not that I was aware. She could have bought some, but Elody had a beautiful set of jade-handled brushes her mother and I gave her the year before my wife died of cancer. They were the only brushes she used because they reminded her of my Patsy." The sorrow in his eyes made my heart hurt.

"Elody tried to send a message before she died. She scrawled the letter T or J. I couldn't really make it out, so it might have just been a random scrawl. Paint spilled across the rest of it and made it unreadable. Other than those things, I have nothing else to add. I'm sorry," I said. I pulled the bottle of wine from the bucket of ice and poured myself a second glass. This was a night in need of calmer nerves than I possessed.

Anthony walked through the open French doors balancing a large plate of char-grilled oysters in garlic sauce in one hand and stuffed mushrooms in the other. The tension slipped away as quickly as it had wormed its way into the evening. "My name is Anthony, and I'll be your server this evening. I present to you a delightful appetizer of oysters and crab-stuffed mushrooms. This mouth-watering gift from the sea is followed by a risotto with sautéed shrimp, pesto and a tomato confit. It's a dish I created and named after myself – Ziggy's Shrimp Pesto Risotto." He placed the appetizers on the table with a small flourish.

"This smells absolutely divine, Anthony!" I sniffed in appreciation. "I haven't eaten this well since…forever!"

"Ziggy's cooking is why I'm forced to run three miles every day at my age. It's the only way to keep my political figure slim and trim." Richard patted his stomach. I had to admit he was in excellent shape for an older man.

"Ziggy? Nickname for Ziegfried?" I asked as I speared an oyster with my appetizer fork and savored the smoky taste of the sea. "Mmmm…these are phenomenal."

"Thank you. Give me a few minutes and I'll be back with the main course. Save one or two for me!" He admonished as he went back inside.

"Anthony's like a son," Richard said. "I had high hopes he and Elody would marry one day, but she wanted someone the complete opposite of her old man. She found him in that criminal she rescued off the street corner." Richard gave a disgusted noise.

"How did she meet him? Please don't be offended, but she partied with the socialites of the state. Jay Burns was an inner city petty crook. He's good looking in a slimy way and charming, but I can't imagine Elody falling for him." I popped a mushroom into my mouth and swore to go to yoga *and* jog if I could eat all the delicious food in front of me.

"You're guess is as good as mine. Anthony dug around in Jay's background. He dropped out of high school after the police arrested him for a string of car thefts tied to gang activity. Because he was a minor, he got off with a slap on the wrist. Cases like his are why my campaign addresses criminals and the lack of appropriate punishment. He stayed out of the criminal system for a year or two, but was arrested at age twenty for hitting his girlfriend. He struck her so hard it broke her nose. He served five years for that assault. I tried to warn Elody, but she swore he wasn't the same man anymore." Richard laid his fork on his plate and shook his head. "I don't understand how such a beautiful, intelligent girl could be won over by the likes of Jay Burns."

"Sir, I can tell you from experience that people do crazy things and ignore obvious signs due to grief or love. If I had to guess, I'd say Elody had a hard time after she lost her mother. Jay nudged a foot into that crack in her emotions and worked his way in without her realizing what was happening," I said. I thought about Shari and how crazed she became after her husband died.

"You're right. Let's talk about something a little less dark. I don't want all this negative talk to ruin the risotto Anthony's bringing." The Senator nodded his chin towards Anthony as he set a steaming dish of risotto and shrimp in the table.

"Let's eat. I've heard the way to a woman's heart is through her stomach, and I aim to see if it's true or not," Anthony joked as he settled himself in the chair next to me.

"If all the food you make is this good, you've got yourself a deal!" I said lightly. "You are an amazing chef."

I shook off the dark thoughts of a moment ago. The night crept across the lake, and stars appeared in the darkening sky. I relaxed a little as the talk turned to stories of campaigns and political blunders. I pushed aside all thoughts of Clint's distance and Elody's murder.

After dinner, Richard took me inside to show me one of Elody's paintings. It was a portrait of a blonde woman with deep, blue eyes and a friendly face. "Was this your wife?" I asked him.

"Yes, this is my beautiful Patsy. She was the most down-to-earth, warm-hearted woman I've ever met. I had twenty-five years with her and I would do anything to be able to spend even one more moment with her."

"She was beautiful," I murmured. I looked closely at the painting. "Elody had considerable talent. This portrait is so lifelike."

"It's the brush strokes. If you look, you can see Elody had a unique way of layering the paint with short, precise brush strokes. When she was ten and her talent first emerged, she spent a summer studying with an amazing teacher in Japan. His technique was different from most painters. Elody learned from a true master," Richard said.

"I'm sorry I never met your daughter. I have a feeling I would have liked her."

"And she would have liked you, too, Phee," Richard said sadly.

CHAPTER TWENTY THREE

At nine o'clock, I asked Anthony to take me home. I had to work in the morning, and the effects of the third glass of wine dulled my brain. I thanked Richard for a wonderful evening and promised I would contact him if I learned anything new. He gave me a hug and closed the door behind us.

Anthony drove slowly away from the lakeside cabin. I leaned back in the seat and enjoyed the music playing on the car stereo. He had interesting taste in music. A 1950s rockabilly tune echoed in the car.

"I know the song but don't recognize the singer," I commented. I had an eclectic taste in music that spanned multiple eras.

"It's my band," Anthony said. "My former band. I'm on the road too much with the campaign, so I had to give it up. Maybe one day I'll rejoin the guys or start another group."

"Is that you singing?" I asked, impressed by another revealed talent.

"No. I play string bass," he answered. "I sing back-up vocals, but I'm not good enough to sing lead. Not by a long shot!"

"You're quite the interesting individual, Ziggy. Senator Campbell is lucky to have you on his team," I said. "He said he hoped you and Elody would get together. She was a beautiful girl. Can I ask why you never dated her?"

"You're right. She was beautiful, but she was also moody and prone to deep depression. I'm a firm believer in *joie de vivre*, and I appreciate life every day. I work hard, but I play harder. I eat and drink the best foods and wines I can afford. I've sky dived in New Zealand and sailed on a boat with my band mates from Maine to Key West, Florida the summer before I started college. My little brother died of leukemia when he was eight, so I don't take life for granted." Anthony gave me a quick glance before returning his eyes to the road ahead. His fingers tapped out a rhythm in time with the song playing. He hummed lightly under his breath.

"I'm sorry about your brother, but you're right. Life is short and sometimes we forget and let the minor bumps in the road bother us. We should get dessert. My motto is life is too short to skip dessert. It doesn't sound as sophisticated as yours, but it works," I smiled at him. I sang along with the CD and Anthony joined in. We rode through the dark night belting out songs as loudly and as off-key as we could.

When we neared town, he slowed. "What's still open at this time of night for dessert?" Anthony asked.

"Nellie Jo's is open until 10 and so is the Quickie Cow. Your call," I answered. "Quickie Cow is about two blocks ahead on the right."

"Quickie Cow it is." He turned his blinker on to turn into the parking lot. Despite the late hour, the little restaurant operating out of a remodeled Silverstream trailer was busy. The summer was the busy season for Carol Ann and Gracie. The sisters stayed open late from May until September to accommodate the crowds. As Anthony eased into a parking spot, I saw Clint sitting at one of the outdoor tables. Across from him sat the blonde I spotted him with earlier. A hot blaze of anger at Clint's infidelity flashed through me. I gripped my hands tightly together to keep from grabbing the door handle and jumping out of the car. I had a momentary vision of running from the car and screaming at him. Fortunately, common sense prevailed. If I made a scene, everyone in town would hear about it before the rooster crowed tomorrow morning. I'd never be able to leave my house again from sheer embarrassment.

"Can I be high maintenance? I'd rather have one of Nellie Jo's mini blueberry pies and a tea if that's okay." I unclasped my hands. My fingernails left small half-moon bites across my palms. I took a deep shuddering breath and calmed myself.

"Sure," Anthony said, giving me a quizzical look. He put the car in reverse, and we headed towards downtown.

The ride to Nellie Jo's was silent except for the music playing in the background. I stewed over Clint's deceit. Maybe I wasted the past twelve plus years of my life mooning over a man incapable of commitment. I was an idiot. Once we parked and entered Nellie Jo's, I kept a tight grip on my emotions. Just twenty minutes before this, I'd had a blast while joking and laughing with Anthony and Richard. I wouldn't allow myself to crumble into a sniveling mess now.

Anthony pulled out my chair for me, then seated himself. Leaning forward, he reached out and touched my hand. "Are you okay? You seem upset about something. I have great listening skills. Comes with the whole aide to a public figure gig." He gave me a half smile.

"You'll think I'm a hot mess if I tell you."

"You are hot, but you're not a mess. Just human. Spill it," Anthony insisted.

"The guy I'm dating was sitting at the Quickie Cow with a woman," I said. I bit my lip and stifled a sob.

"Did you recognize the girl?"

"No, but it's the same girl I saw him with earlier today. I'm a fool," I sighed.

"You could be jumping to conclusions," he said. At the skeptical raise of my eyebrows, he continued, "If he drove by here and saw you sitting at the table with me, how would it look? You need to talk to the guy. Give him the benefit of the doubt."

I thought about what he said as Missy, the college student who worked for Nellie Jo in the summer, took our order of blueberry mini-pies. I asked for an herbal tea blend. Anthony ordered a blueberry cream coffee, and I grimaced. "What? I like to walk on the wild side with my food and drink choices. It will be the best coffee I've ever had," he declared. I remained doubtful.

"You're probably right. Clint's an honest guy. I'll ask him who she is. Thanks for listening," I said. There had to be an explanation. Clint might be a lot of things, but I'd never known him to cheat on anyone he dated. I was acting like a jealous shrew which was the kind of person I promised myself to never be. Clint didn't play games with people's emotions. Juliet had planted a small doubt in my head, and I'd taken it to heart.

Missy set our order down in front of us with the check. Anthony pulled out a twenty and told her to keep the change. Turning back to me, he said, "You're welcome. Dear Abby used to call on me for advice."

"When you were what? Five? Nice try!" I laughed. I took a bite of my blueberry pie. Delicious. "Can I ask you a few things about Elody?"

"Sure. I'll answer what I can. I had little to do with her in the past few years. She was away at college and then living on her own when she dropped out. She and Richard had a falling out over her drinking and public antics about a year ago."

"The gossip columns said Elody used drugs. Could she have crossed the wrong person, and her death is related to her partying?" I asked. I blew on my tea to cool it down before taking a sip.

"Elody didn't do drugs. She drank a little too much, but she was rabid about people who took drugs of any kind. If the press can't find news, they make it up. A senator's kid on drugs sells papers regardless of the truth," Anthony said. He sipped his coffee. His eyes lit up. "This is amazing. You need to try it."

"Ugh. I couldn't swallow blueberry-flavored coffee if you paid me. I'll take your word for it." I swallowed another bite of pie. "So no drugs. What about the people she partied with in the city? I'm sure you or the senator ran background checks on all of her friends. Don't deny it."

"He did. A few of them smoked pot, but most of her friends were disgruntled debutantes with too much money and time on their hands. They drank and stayed up all night dancing at clubs, but they were fairly benign. Jay, on the other hand, is a criminal and a thug. Personally, I believe he killed Elody, but how do I prove it?" Anthony asked.

CHAPTER TWENTY FOUR

Anthony and I sat in silence as we finished the last few bites of our pie. I wasn't surprised that Anthony thought Jay killed Elody. I hadn't discovered any clear motive for killing the twenty-three year old. A lover's quarrel gone wrong made sense. He and Senator Campbell could be correct in their suspicions, but I wondered if they had blinders on when it came to other possible suspects.

"What about Tessa Brewer, the reporter?" I asked. "She's been like an attack Chihuahua with her articles about Elody. She treads a thin line between slander and news with her past articles regarding drug use with Elody's crowd."

"Tessa Brewer is just like any of these other jackals circling the governor waiting for an opportunity to feast. I don't even pay attention to her articles and neither should you. She's a hack," Anthony deemed. "She's a fan of Jay Burns' art which should tell you a little about her opinions and her taste. Tessa Brewer carries a torch for Jay and attacked Elody's reputation out of jealousy."

"My sister, Juliet, and I ate lunch with Jay today. He seemed distraught over Elody whenever someone mentioned her or when the cameras were pointed at him. The rest of the time, I felt like he was mentally undressing me. It's nothing I can put my finger on, but Jay's the type of guy who uses people to survive." I sipped the last of my tea and set the cup on the table. "I'd better get home. Summer reading will kill me this year if I don't get some rest. I have double the number of children signed up as last year. It's great for the kids and the library, but it keeps me running to make sure shelves are restocked with books and enough crafts are available for the families."

We stood up and after waving goodbye to Missy, headed towards Anthony's car. As we cruised down Main Street, I thought about the other people close to Elody. "What do you think about Elody's college roommate, Shawna Collins? Their neighbor at the lake overheard Shawna and Elody arguing one night. From what the neighbor said, the argument sounded heated. Shawna accused Elody of being stupid about something. Shawna said she planned to handle things if Elody didn't."

"Shawna's a good egg," Anthony said. "She was right to be upset with Elody. Shawna came by the Senator's office a few weeks before Elody dropped off the social radar. According to her, Jay slapped Elody one night so hard it bruised her face. Elody refused to say what the fight was about and wouldn't press charges. Shawna wanted us to throw Jay in jail. Unfortunately, it's not that easy to do even for a bigwig in Congress. A week or so later, Elody moved out of Jay's loft and came here, so we didn't pursue it. Now I wished we had," Anthony said, a guilty frown on his face.

"I wonder if Elody planned to go back to Jay and Shawna tried to talk her out of it. It would explain why the fight escalated. Love, even misguided love, makes people do stupid things," I said. "You missed my house. If you turn right here, we can just go around the block."

Anthony swung the wheel and made a quick right. As he took another right around the backside of my block, I saw a dark figure heading across Mr. Chambray's backyard and towards mine.

"Slow down!" I barked, startling Anthony and causing him to slam on the brakes. "Is that someone sneaking into my backyard?" I pointed in the direction of the dark shape.

"I'm not sure but let's find out." Anthony sped up and as he came closer to my house, he turned his headlights off and eased the sedan into park a few houses down from mine. "Let's go. Stay behind me." He reached into his glove box and pulled out a gun. He tucked it into the back of his belt.

"A gun? Is that necessary?" I asked, shocked and a little frightened that this funny, suave guy carried a handgun. It seemed against his nature.

"The Senator receives threats every day. All of his close, long-term staffers have concealed carry permits. If someone sneaks through a yard late at night, they aren't there to deliver Girl Scout cookies. If you're scared, you're welcome to wait in the car," Anthony offered. The light-hearted charmer of earlier had disappeared and in his place was a steely-eyed professional.

"I'll wait here. Be careful," I warned. Anthony slipped out of the car and pushed the door shut without a sound. He slid into the dark and out of sight.

I waited with my hand poised above the emergency call button on my phone. I debated whether I should call the Sheriff or wait to see what Anthony discovered. The minutes ticked by and just when I convinced myself to call, Anthony emerged from the side of my house holding someone. A hoodie covered the person's face. He shoved the person roughly in front of him. I jumped out of the car and rushed towards them.

"Someone decided to do some late night snooping in your backyard," Anthony said. He let go and pulled the hood down from Tessa Brewer's face.

I gasped in shock. "Tessa Brewer! What in Sam Hill are you doing sneaking into my yard? I'm calling the sheriff."

"Wait! I just wanted to get some pictures without you knowing it. I heard you were the one who discovered Elody's body. I'm just trying to make a living here. Everybody needs to chill out." Tessa's voice slipped into an Arkansas drawl and she lost her sophisticated demeanor under my angry gaze.

"You're lucky I didn't call them already," I admonished her. "Go home, Tessa. Take your mean-spirited gossip and innuendos about folks and go home." I was tired and had enough of this whole sordid mess for one night.

"There's a nugget of truth behind every item I report," Tessa said with a nasty laugh. "Elody Campbell wasn't the sainted angel she appeared. She squandered her talent and didn't appreciate how easy her life was. Some people have to work hard to get ahead. Not everyone is born with a silver spoon in their mouth."

"Go home," I repeated. "Anthony, thank you again for a lovely evening. I'll call you if I learn anything new."

"Get some rest, Phee. I'll make sure she leaves," Anthony gave Tessa a slight push towards the street.

I trudged up my front steps and unlocked my door. Stumbling to my bedroom and into my pajamas, I was asleep before my head hit my pillow.

CHAPTER TWENTY FIVE

The next morning when my alarm went off, I cursed the extra glass of wine I drank with dinner. Exhausted and cranky from so little sleep, I showered and dragged my sad sack self to the library. Charlie waited outside for me. Today was the day he took the garbage out and helped clean.

"Hey there, pretty lady. Don't take this wrong, but you look like something not even my cat would bother dragging in," Charlie said. He followed behind me as I unlocked the doors. He grabbed the garbage pail nearest the front door and took it with him to empty into the large can.

"I feel even worse," I grumbled. "I ate dinner with Senator Campbell last night. My one glass of wine turned into three. I'm not equipped to handle a good time."

"Senator Campbell, huh? He's here because of his daughter's murder, isn't he? I've never seen so many dang reporters in my life. You'd think we lived in the big city between the murder and the press. Darn ridiculous!" Charlie shook his head. "I can't wait until things get back to normal."

There was a light tapping on the front door of the library. I hurried to the front thinking Wade forgot his keys. It was Clint. Next to him was the short blonde from yesterday. I unlocked the doors to let him in.

"Good morning, babe. I brought you coffee. You look tired. Are you feeling okay?" He leaned in and kissed me. "I also brought Lu by to meet you before we have our cookout tonight."

The blonde woman stepped forward and held out her hand. "Lucinda Gifford, but my friends call me Lu. I'm Clint's new partner," she said. I took her outreached hand and gave her a quick once-over. Lu had blonde hair and dark brown eyes. Up close, I could see freckles sprinkled across her golden-colored skin. A snub nose and too wide mouth made her appear cute and perky rather than pretty. Despite her short stature, she had the stance of a fighter that could wrestle an unruly drunk to the ground with no problem. I couldn't decide if I should be jealous or scared of her.

"Nice to meet you, Lucinda," I said. I took the coffee from Clint's outstretched hand and sipped it gratefully.

"Please call me Lu. I feel like I've known you forever since Clint's talked nonstop about you since we met," Lu said with an accent I couldn't quite pinpoint.

"Where are you from originally, Lu?" I asked.

"Queens. You couldn't tell from my accent? Born and raised in the big city. This is my first trip to someplace without a subway and a taxi on every corner. I'm in culture shock."

"I've lived here with my family my entire life. In fact, Clint spent more time at my house then he did at his own. We'll help you navigate small town life," I offered. I couldn't help but let my guard down now that I'd met her. Something about Lu told me she was an ally rather than a rival. Despite coming from the big city, her smile held small town charm. It made me glad I hadn't made a scene and embarrassed myself yesterday. "What made you move here?"

"I'm hiding from a mob boss who wants to take me out," Lu said grimly. When she saw the shock on my face, she burst into laughter. "I'm yanking your chain, Phee. My dad's a cop and my three brothers are cops. I wanted to forge my own path without the men in my family hovering over me. Three generations of Irish-American cops. If that ain't a stereotype, I don't know what is."

"It sounds like police work is in your blood," I smiled at her.

"Yep. Stopping crime is what the Gifford family lives, breathes and bleeds. My dad met my mom when he slapped cuffs on her one day," Lu said.

"What did she do?" I asked, scared to hear the answer as various scenarios flitted through my mind.

"She was working a street corner..." Lu said. "Just kidding. You're right, Clint. She's an easy one to get going. Nah, she was protesting a business in the city that discriminated against Hispanics. Mom's Puerto Rican. She's a labor law attorney, a hippie and an activist. My dad's a die-hard cop who walks the straight and narrow. How my parents married is beyond me. As you can see, I got my looks from my dad, but my sense of humor is all from my mom."

Clint wrapped an arm around my shoulder. "Phee, Lu's driving me nuts. I'll need your help to keep up with all of her practical jokes."

"Oh, I'll be helping her, not you. Someone needs to keep you on your toes," I joked. "Lu, come meet Charlie. He is a town icon. Knows everything about everything. He's a huge Cincinnati Reds fan, too."

"I'll enlighten him to the error of his ways. New York Yankees all the way." Lu followed me to the office. I introduced her to Charlie and left them bickering over team stats.

"Time for a proper hello," Clint whispered huskily. He leaned down and gave me a deep kiss. "I've missed you."

"I've missed you, too," I whispered and rested my head on his chest. "It's been a rough few days."

"I'm sorry, sweetheart. I wish I'd been here to help." He stroked my curls and pulled me tighter to him. I leaned back and looked up at his face. He smiled and his eyes crinkled in the corners. "What? Have I got mud on my face and no one's told me?"

Juliet's words from the other day echoed in my head, but I shoved them away. Clint didn't do over-the-top romantic gestures or behave like a storybook prince, but I knew he loved me. "Nothing. I'm tired is all. Late night eating dinner with Senator Campbell, then when his aide, Anthony, dropped me off at my house, we found a reporter lurking in my back yard. Tessa Brewer tried to sneak up to my windows to take pictures of me. Someone let it slip I was the one who found the body."

"Damn it, Phee, you should've called me. I don't want to depend on the senator's lapdog to keep you safe, but I'm glad you're okay. I'm sure more nuts will drop from the trees before we solve this case. If she shows up again, call me. How else am I going to play macho boyfriend and save the day?" He smiled at me. "The sheriff discovered that a tech at the crime lab in Burlington owed the wrong person money and leaked information to anyone with a fat wallet. That's probably where Tessa found out about you. The lab fired him."

"Good. The Senator said he learned information by greasing someone's palm with cash. It's a shame so many people's lives are motivated by money," I sighed. "Clearly I am not driven by cash since I work at a library. My love of books is what I live on."

"We can't all live off love, great movies, and books," Clint admonished with a playful chuck under my chin.

"I like money just as much as the next person, but I also realize it isn't everything," I grumbled. "It sickens me when people trade away their values and damage other people's lives for it."

"I agree with you one hundred percent. I promise to never tell any reporter you wear skunk slippers and sheep pajamas to bed. I find them incredibly arousing, but others might be appalled at your skunk slaying ways," Clint joked. "I'd hate for some skunk activist to stalk you if your dirty secret was splashed across the front pages of the newspaper."

"Ha ha. You deserve Lu and her practical jokes, you brat!" I gave him a playful push. "I need to get ready to open the doors. You need to skedaddle out of here and go catch a murderer."

"You're right. The sheriff is getting pressure from all sides to arrest someone for Elody's murder. Signs are pointing to Jay Burns, but with no hard evidence against him, we can't do it. It's not a crime to be slime. I'll check out this Tessa Brewer character. I don't like her lurking around in the bushes. Paparazzi or not, it sounds suspicious."

"Check out her rap sheet in Arkansas. I found out she was the getaway driver for her dad in a string of robberies. It looks like she straightened out her life since her release from juvie, but maybe she hasn't given up all her criminal antics. I'm sure they come in handy when stalking a star," I informed him. "I better get busy. I'll see you and Lu tonight. Okay if Wade and Juliet come?"

"Great idea. See you at six. I'll bring my grill apron and charm," Clint said. He gave me another quick, hard kiss and walked away. Lu pried herself away from her heated conversation about baseball with Charlie and followed behind him.

Charlie and I finished cleaning the library. Wade arrived fifteen minutes before we opened and helped to shelve the books left in the book drop. At ten o'clock, we opened the doors. Between summer readers and our usual patrons, I didn't have time to worry about anything but books, crafts and reading logs.

In the afternoon, Juliet popped her head around the shelf where I was straightening books. "Hey there, PheePhee. Time for lunch and investigating lies and alibis."

"Oh! You scared me!" I squeaked. I glanced at my watch. "You're right. I promised to meet Shawna for lunch. Are you coming with me?"

"I planned to go with you. My interrogation techniques need honing. Each perp sharpens my skills and hardens my heart. If Clint would let me slap cuffs on some scumbag, my life would be complete."

"Instead of a 'Y' on your mask, perhaps you should bedazzle it with an 'F'," I suggested.

"What for?" Juliet wrinkled her forehead in confusion.

"For Super Freak," I laughed and pushed her towards the door.

CHAPTER TWENTY SIX

Juliet took pity upon my exhaustion and drove me to the Quickie Cow. On the way, I told her about the events of the night before. When we arrived, I saw Shawna sitting at one of the tables with a large umbrella. She already had her lunch in front of her.

"I hope you don't mind. I got here early. I couldn't take the smell of French fries a second longer, so I went ahead and ordered," Shawna apologized. She swirled her fries in a glob of catsup and stuffed them in her mouth.

"I understand. Their fries are the best," I agreed. Juliet and I both ordered a jalapeño burger with fries and a peach shake. Good thing I promised to go to yoga and take up jogging. My calorie count from the past few days was through the roof. I liked my curves, but didn't want to split another pair of yoga pants. After our order came up, we carried our burger baskets and shakes to Shawna's table.

"Thanks for inviting me to lunch," Shawna said. She slurped her soda and emitted a small burp. "Sorry. Carbonation kills me every single time. I'm at a loss since Elody's death. I want to stick around to help catch the killer, but the artsy crowd is plucking at my last nerve. Give me a microscope and I'm in heaven. A paintbrush gives me the willies."

"But you liked Elody's art, didn't you?" Juliet asked.

"Yes, but she was my friend. Otherwise, I wouldn't have wasted my time on it," Shawna admitted. "She had talent, but as far as knowing style and technique, I'm at a loss. I cared because she cared. With Elody gone, if I don't go to another art gallery, I'd survive."

Her blunt honesty reinforced my original assessment that she cared about Elody. Even so, I wanted to pry deeper into their relationship and the fight the neighbor overheard. "Shawna, a neighbor said you and Elody argued before she died. What did you guys fight about?" I asked.

Shawna stuffed a few more fries into her mouth. Not waiting to swallow, she talked around the mush of fries, "We fought over Jay. The scumbag slapped her after she confronted him about using her to make money. I wanted her to press charges, but she didn't want to ruin his life when he was trying to go legit."

"How was Jay using her to make money?" I asked. I took a bite of my burger. A jalapeño set my mouth on fire. I grabbed my shake and took a quick sip. Gasping, I said, "Didn't he make money off the sales of his art?"

"I'm not sure. I heard her arguing with him on the phone one day. She said he wouldn't be where he was with his career if not for her. She called him a two-bit hack and threatened to tell all the newspapers about him. I asked her about it, but she brushed me off. I demanded she tell me. It went downhill from there," Shawna. "I feel like crap for pushing the issue."

"Have the police made any progress figuring out who broke into your cabin?" Juliet asked.

"No. A few stolen paintings don't compare to solving the mystery of who killed the artist. They didn't take anything else. My computer was on the table and Elody had some expensive pieces of jewelry, but the robber didn't touch either," Shawna said. She heaved a sigh and her eyes glistened with tears. "Everything is falling apart. I fought with Elody and never made up with her. I wished that I had handled it better. I'm like the bull in the china shop. I break things, then can't glue them back together."

"We all have moments like that. Things we wish we could undo or words we could take back," Juliet reassured her. "I'm sure Elody knew you cared about her."

"I really did. She made me take a break from books and beakers. If not for her, I wouldn't have gone to a frat party or learned to skateboard. Elody was a blast as a friend. Now that she's gone, I'll be plain old boring Shawna, the science geek," Shawna sighed and took another loud slurp of her soda. She sat glumly staring at her empty basket.

"You can come visit us," Juliet offered. "We're a hoot, Phee and I."

"We are?" Juliet might be a hoot, but I was more of a small chirp. "I mean, yes, we'd love to have you visit. I've got a spare room. You're welcome anytime."

"Really? You're not saying that because you feel sorry for me?" Shawna looked like a puppy waiting to receive a treat for going potty outside. If she had a tail, she would have wagged it.

"Sure. You can join us on girls' night out this Thursday. I invited Willow, so we need a fourth to balance us out. Besides, Phee's a book nerd and needs someone like her to keep her company. It'll be fun, you'll see," Juliet promised.

"Cool. Thanks a lot. I better get back to the cabin. I'm writing up my notes from last semester and working on my paper. It's a beast, so a break later this week would be awesome!" Shawna stood up and dumped her napkins and empty drink into the nearby trash. She set the empty basket on the counter and walked away with a little skip to her step. Making new friends seemed to have added spark to Shawna's personality.

Juliet leaned forward and said in a low voice, "We need to find out how Jay was making money off of Elody. It had to be through her art. She didn't have any money since Daddy Dearest cut her off."

"We should talk to Nicolette over at Stone Street Gallery on our way back. She might have insight into the wheeling and dealing of Jay Burns. Forewarning, she thinks we should leave investigating crime to the cops, so tread lightly," I warned.

"I'll be undercover. I'll be so deep into my role, she won't even recognize me."

"Just act calm, cool and collected and let me do most of the talking. Somehow we need to see the paintings Elody left at the gallery for Nic to sell. I think they're the key to breaking this whole case wide open," I predicted. I sipped my peach shake still trying to ease the heat of the burger's jalapenos.

CHAPTER TWENTY SEVEN

Juliet and I parked in front of Stone Street Gallery. The heat of the afternoon sun reflected off the windows of the building. I opened the door and enjoyed the rush of cool air as it washed over me. Juliet and I walked in and looked for Nicolette. The gallery had the same quiet stillness I associated with museums.

"Hello. Can I help you?" A young man stepped out from behind the front desk to greet us.

"Is Nicolette around? I wanted to look at some paintings she told me she recently acquired," I said. I looked around at the paintings gracing the stark white walls.

"She's gone to run a few errands, then she's off to meet with the artist Jay Burns. He's offering us the chance to sell two of his final paintings. I'm so excited, I could burst!" He clapped his hands together in excitement and gave a little hop.

"No wonder you're excited. That will give the gallery great exposure," Juliet said.

"You aren't kidding. Nic and I've been running around like crazy trying to make sure the gallery is in tip-top shape for when we highlight his pieces. Oh, gracious. I'm being rude. I'm Kevin." He held his hand out to shake mine.

"You look familiar. Weren't you a year or two behind me in school?" Juliet asked, squinting at him. "Kevin Ratcliff! I knew I recognized you. It's so good to see you. I thought you moved away."

"I did, but the lake and this community have always been my muse," Kevin said. "I came back to do a series of wood carvings inspired by the wildlife in the area. I work here part-time for Nic."

"The gallery looks great," I said, making a show of admiring the space. "Could you point us in the direction of the paintings Nic was telling me about? They were painted by Elody Campbell. I wanted a chance to see them after Nic gushed over how talented she was. Such a waste."

Kevin shook his shaggy head in sympathy, "It's terrible. She showed some serious talent. Too bad she copied another artist's style."

"Whose style did she copy?" Juliet asked.

"Jay Burns, of course. It's understandable. They were in a relationship and probably shared a studio. I'm sure he mentored and encouraged her. Some artists have a hard time moving from mimic to master. Elody was still in the infant stages of her art career," Kevin said. "I can show you her paintings though. They are in the back since we planned to wrap them up this afternoon. Her father came in and bought all of them."

"It's understandable he'd want his daughter's art. It gives him something to remember her," Juliet said sagely.

Kevin took us to a workroom in the back and steered us towards a long table. Three paintings rested atop it. I moved in and examined Elody's art. Her work was amazing. The water scene that lay in front of me practically made me smell the ocean and hear the waves crashing against the rocky shore as gulls screamed above the water.

"She really had talent," I said. "Is it okay if I pick this painting up and examine it closer?"

"Just be careful," Kevin said.

"Kevin, my sister works with rare books and is used to working with objects that need special handling. I'll vouch for her," Juliet said. "Can you show me some of the pieces around here? Are any of your carvings at the gallery?" Juliet tucked her arm into his and led him towards the front. Glancing over her shoulder, she winked at me. Message received.

I quickly picked up the painting in front of me and examined it closely. These paintings had the same distinct brush stroke her father showed me. I turned the painting over. On the back was a paper with Elody's name, the title of the painting and a date from over four years ago. I wondered if that was the date the piece was completed. Curious, I examined the other two paintings on the table. Each was dated close to four years ago. These paintings must have been ones she finished prior to her mother's death. According to the gossip columns I found, Elody and Jay had been dating almost a year. She hadn't imitated him. It appeared that the exact opposite was true. That must be why she accused him of being a hack. I leaned closer and examined the paintings again. All three were definitely by the same artist. I saw a small EC painted in the far right corner of each – Elody Campbell.

"Kevin, you are still a hoot," Juliet said loudly as they strolled back to where I stood.

"Juliet, I hate to tear you away, but I've got to return to work before Wade thinks I'm never coming back," I said.

"Thank you for showing me these paintings. They are stunning."

"Anytime. Come back and see us when we acquire Jay's pieces."

Juliet and I hurried back to her car. As she drove me to the library, I told her what I'd found. "So I think Jay Burns imitated Elody's painting style and made money off of it," I concluded.

"Jay could've used Elody's contacts to help jumpstart his career even if he wasn't that talented. She had connections to wealthy families and art collectors across the state. Why would he need to imitate her style?"

"I'm not sure, but those paintings were dated prior to the start of their relationship. I could be wrong, but we should dig a little deeper into Jay's sudden skyrocket to fame," I said. "If I'm right, it happened at the same time he met Elody. She was already on the outs with her dad. Her relationship with Jay slammed shut the family's coffers and its connections."

"While you're pushing books on unsuspecting children and parents, I'll get online at the library and search through the newspaper archives. I'll see what I can discover on our mysteriously talented Jay," Juliet said. "My investigative skills go from boardroom to keyboard in the blink of an eye."

"Oh, sheesh! Give it a rest with the bad cop lingo," I laughed.

"Just keepin' it real and keepin' our suspect in the crosshairs." Juliet slipped a pair of mirrored sunglasses on and began to sing at the top of her lungs, "Bad boys, bad boys, whatchoo gonna do? Whatchoo gonna do when Phee comes for you?"

I sank lower in the seat of the convertible and prayed no one could hear her. Thank goodness the ride to the library was short and her tune ended before we arrived.

CHAPTER TWENTY EIGHT

Juliet and I parted ways once inside the library. She went to the bank of computers along our back wall to get the skinny on our skeevy artist. I headed to the children's area to help Matt Grayson choose books. He only read science fiction and had consumed most of my newer books. I helped him locate some older books that caught his interest, then spent several minutes straightening the shelves and picking up board books strewn across the floor by easily distracted toddlers.

I took over the circulation desk for Wade so he could stretch his legs. Since being fitted for artificial limbs, he made a point to move more often and keep his thigh muscles limber. It also helped to toughen the scarred skin where the knees fitted to the artificial limbs. I was focused on checking in a large stack of recently returned books when I heard a quiet cough. Tessa Brewer stood in front of me. Startled at her sudden appearance, I snapped, "Can I help you?"

"I came to tell you I'm sorry. I acted like a common thief sneaking through your backyard. It was unprofessional and uncalled for and I want to apologize," Tessa said.

"You're lucky I didn't call the police." I glared across the desk at her. I didn't entirely believe her apology. Realizing I lied to her during our previous run-in at the park, I reigned in my anger and adopted a simpering tone. "Not that I would have actually called them once I realized it was you. It was actually pretty exciting to know a big time reporter like you wanted to talk to me." I almost batted my eyelashes at her, but stopped the impulse in time.

"Can I ask you a few questions about discovering Elody?"

The snake moved in for the strike just like I knew she would. "I don't know anything more than what Sheriff Dawes said in his press conference. I wish I could be more help to you."

"Why were you in the park at daybreak? Isn't that a little odd?" Tessa leaned across the circulation desk and fixed me with an intense stare.

I gave a fake little giggle. "Oh gosh. You don't understand the work that goes into setting up a book sale. I arrived early to set up tables and unload boxes. Elody had been dead awhile before I arrived. It was awful."

"Interesting. So you got a good look at the body?"

Her pushy questions made me uncomfortable. I could see how she would be a good reporter though. Her direct, in-your-face questions made me feel like a suspect under the heat lamps. "I had a brief glimpse. I realized right away that she was dead, so I went back to my van and called the police." I shrugged and adopted a vacant look.

"No evidence of who killed her? Nothing?" Tessa practically lay across the top of the desk as she peppered me with questions.

"Nope," I shook my head. "I'm sorry, but I need to help Mrs. Short." I looked over her shoulder at Mrs. Short who stood behind Tessa with a stack of books. Tessa looked annoyed, but stepped aside. She turned and wandered off.

"I could've waited, but you looked like a kitten cornered by a big dog. I figured I'd rescue you," Mrs. Short whispered.

"Thanks. She's one of the reporters camped out while they investigate the murder. I hope the police solve it so they'll all crawl back under their rocks."

"Amen. I could barely find a parking spot this morning." Ann Short worked as a nurse at our small medical clinic.

I finished checking out her books and after chatting about the possibility of Founder's Day being rescheduled, I told her I'd talk to her later. I opened up the drawer next to the computer to grab a fresh roll of receipt tape for our date due printer. As I pulled out the tape, I realized I had ink all over my fingers. Glancing in the drawer, I found that a pen had exploded. Ink was everywhere. "Dang. Glad I didn't wear white pants," I grumbled. "Wade, can you watch the desk for a minute? I've got ink all over me, and I need to wash it off. Can you grab something to clean this mess up, too? Thanks."

I hurried into the ladies room. I scrubbed my hands under the water and the water went from blue to clear after a few minutes. As I dried my hands, a stall door opened and Tessa stepped out. "Oh, hello," she said. "Don't worry. I'm not going to ask you any questions."

"It's okay. Can I ask you a few?" Since I had her in front of me, it couldn't hurt to turn the tables. "Like I said before, I read all of your columns. I can tell you covered all the news about Elody, but what do you know about her boyfriend, Jay Burns? I met him at the lake yesterday. What a sweetie. He seemed heartbroken over Elody's murder."

Tessa had been applying a bright red lipstick in the mirror, but at my mention of Jay, her hand paused. She smacked her lips together and closed her lipstick tube. Taking her time, she opened her purse and dropped the tube in. She snapped the purse shut with an angry motion and it tipped over. The contents rolled across the counter. With a snort of annoyance, she swept up the spilled items to push them back in. When she did, I saw the butt of a gun sticking out. I suppressed a gasp. I leaned towards the mirror and pretended to fluff my curls.

"Jay is a talented artist. I discovered him painting outside one day while Elody gadded about with her groupies playing volleyball. I managed to strike up a conversation with him. After he showed me a few more pieces, I offered to show them to an art critic friend at the paper. One thing led to another and now he's getting the credit he deserves. It's unfortunate that he's decided to give up painting because of Elody's death."

"Maybe your coverage of the club scene wasn't a total waste of your amazing writing talent," I cooed. "You launched Jay's career. If he makes it as an actor, he'll remember you and return the favor."

"Oh, I think I can predict that Jay and I will cross paths again in the future," Tessa said mysteriously. "I'd better run. If there isn't a break in the case soon, I'm going to jet out of this one horse town and head back to the city. I need to go nose around at the sheriff's office and see if there's an update. Sorry again about last night." She picked her purse up off of the counter and slung it across her shoulder. As the door eased slowly shut behind her, I sucked in a deep breath and calmed my nerves. I couldn't believe she carried a gun. She did live in the city which had more crime, but it still shocked me. I'm glad she didn't have her purse with her last night when she crept through my yard. As I flashed back to the previous evening, a thought dawned. Tessa didn't have anything on her last night. For someone who hoped to take a picture of me, shouldn't she have carried a camera? I bit my lip and realized we needed to look deeper into the lives of both Jay and Tessa.

I exited the restroom and hurried over to Juliet. "Holy tuna fish rotting in the sun! Tessa Brewer's got a gun!"

"What? Are you pulling my leg? What's a reporter doing packing heat? Maybe she shoots more than candid camera shots."

"She came here under the pretense of apologizing for last night, but then she tried to weasel information out of me. She claims she discovered Jay," I said and sat down in the chair next to Juliet.

"She was the first reporter to write about him," Juliet said. She clicked on a link and showed me an article she'd found. "I found something else you might find of interest."

She opened another page that was an in-depth article about Jay by Phil Padgett, style editor. When I finished reading it, I leaned back and stared at Juliet in shock. Jay Burns had lived in the same small Arkansas town as Tessa until his family moved when he was ten. I shifted from Miss Marple mode to Sherlock Holmes and examined the evidence Juliet and I uncovered thus far. "Everything in this world is relative, my dear Juliet."

"You're not kidding. It's a small world after all."

CHAPTER TWENTY NINE

Closing time came soon enough. I locked up the library with Wade and told him I'd see him shortly. He and Juliet planned to come early and start the grill for the burgers and kabobs. I swung by the bakery to pick up a chocolate raspberry cake with a dark chocolate ganache for dessert. By five thirty, I had changed into a pair of capris with a sleeveless top of cobalt blue, had placed the beer and wine on ice on the back porch, and started a pasta salad. A few minutes before six, Juliet and Wade arrived. While Wade lit the grill, Juliet and I poured ourselves glasses of white wine and plopped onto my wicker chairs to supervise.

"I want to meet this Lu chick and make sure she doesn't have designs on Clint," Juliet said. "You're far too trusting of the fairer sex."

"Yes, because we women are oh so evil," I said with a wry smile. "You realize you're a woman, too, right?"

"If you aren't sure if you are, I can help out with that question," Wade called out from the yard where he stood waiting to place the kabobs on the grill.

"Hardy har har, Wade. I know I'm a girl. I also realize that not all women care if a man is in a relationship. I'm here to assist my big sister in scoping out the competition," Juliet announced.

"If I have to be jealous all the time, then I don't need to be with Clint. Life and love shouldn't be that hard," I said as I took a sip of wine. "I'll admit I get a twinge of jealousy, but I don't want to turn into one of those women you see on the talk shows who pull hair and curse up a storm over their man. Besides, Clint and I are grown adults and can handle our insecurities in a calm and rational manner."

"You crack me up. I can't believe you actually said that with a straight face. I think you believe it, too. Calm and rational. Ha! Clint's a great guy, but now and then, a girl needs to do a relationship tune-up. Is everything cruising along smoothly, or do you need to do a wash and a wax to make sure he doesn't trade you in for a newer model," Juliet advised in a serious voice.

"I'm not listening to your advice, little sister. Wade's the longest relationship you've been in, and he's amazing. What's up with all the negative talk about relationships?"

Juliet sat silently sipping her wine before she spoke. "I'm sorry. I'm probably being hard on Clint because I'm in a pickle myself. Wade's been hinting about marriage and when we have kids. It's freaking me out. I don't know if I'm ready for a house, a mortgage, two point five kids and a dog named Spike."

"Have you told Wade how you feel?" I asked.

"No. He's the greatest guy, and I don't want to risk losing him."

"I think Wade will understand. As long as you tell him that you are more of a tortoise than a hare in the relationship race, he'll be fine. If you act like a jerk and break up with him, though, I'll have tortoise soup for dinner," I nudged her bare foot with mine. "Talk to him. He'll understand."

"I will. I'd apologize to Clint for being a jerk to him, but since he didn't even know it…" Juliet said. "Speaking of him, I think I hear his truck."

A moment later, Clint walked out the kitchen door followed by Lu. "Girl, I love your house. I thought Clint exaggerated when he described it to me, but it's amazing. I'd love it if you could give me a few pointers on my new place. I'm a pressed wood and futon woman, but I'm willing to trade it all in if my place could look like yours," Lu said. She turned to Juliet. "Hi. I'm Lu. You must be Juliet and that good-looking grill guy must be Wade. Clint's told me all about you."

"Nice to meet you," Juliet said. She stood up and walked towards the tub of iced drinks. "Can I get you something to drink? A glass of wine, beer, water?"

"Just water for me, thanks."

Clint stepped over to my chair and leaned down to kiss me. "I've been counting down the minutes until I could see you again," he whispered.

I gazed up at him and touched my hand to his dark stubble and kissed him back. "I've missed you, too. I'm glad you're back."

"Oh, you two lovebirds are the cutest thing since Cabbage Patch dolls," Lu joked. "I need to find myself a boyfriend and even up the odds here."

"Miller's Cove isn't exactly a dating hotspot. Pickings were already slim. When Juliet snapped me up, it left only the dregs. Sorry." Wade gave a goofy grin and winked at her as he walked up on the porch. "Phee told me you came here from New York. Not nearly the same crime here as you'd find there. You don't think you'll get bored?"

"From the looks of things, Miller's Cove is moving up in the crime world. A minor celebrity found dead in the park. What's not to love about being a cop here?"

"Lu, I think you and I are going to get along great," Juliet declared. "I might need to pick your brain about what it's like to be a female cop. I'm tossing around the idea of going to the police academy."

My head whipped around so fast that I almost got whiplash. "Put the glass down and step away from the wine bottle, lady. You've clearly had too much to drink already. What are you talking about, Juls? You realize cops carry guns and aren't into the whole peace, love and karma business, right? You can't walk up to a criminal, stick a flower in his hair and call the case closed."

"Duh. I know all this, thank you very much. Shari going nuts and now this latest murder has really made me think about how I can make a difference. I've learned everything I can about law enforcement the past six months, and I'm intrigued. I'm considering my life opportunities and not closing any doors," Juliet said with a lofty sniff of her nose.

"We haven't even figured out who killed Elody yet, so our detecting skills might not be up to par." I couldn't believe Juliet thought she should go into law enforcement. This might be her most hare-brained idea ever. I couldn't wait to tell Rick this latest one.

"Wait a minute. You two are trying to solve this murder? Who are you? Nancy Drew and her sidekick

Betsy?" Lu asked. "I mean, don't you think you ought to leave the investigating to the professionals?"

"Bess," Juliet and I corrected automatically. I continued, "I found the body. We've asked a few questions around town. Nothing major. It's more satisfying our idle curiosity than really investigating."

"We've done more than ask a few questions, Phee. Don't be so modest," Juliet said, ignoring my pointed looks and dodging my poorly-aimed kick to her ankle. "Tessa Brewer has a gun in her purse and as you both know, Elody was shot, not stabbed. Jay Burns and Tessa grew up in the same small town in Arkansas. Coincidence? I think not. Shawna Collins, Elody's college roommate, fought with Elody about her not turning Jay into the police for hitting her. Not bad for untrained professionals." Juliet leaned back with a smug look on her face. Wade, sensing a storm brewing with Juliet and Clint, hopped off the porch to pull the meat off the grill.

"I'm not even getting into this right now since I don't want to ruin our evening. After what happened last year with Phee, I would hope you two would have gained an ounce of common sense," Clint said tightly.

"What?" I sputtered. "I'm sorry. Did you just say what I think you said?"

Clint heaved a sigh. "I just came across as an overbearing ass, didn't I?"

"Uh, yeah, you sure did," Lu said with an incredulous expression. "Women are just as capable of taking care of ourselves as men are. We don't need a big, strong he-man bossing us around. Do we, ladies?"

Juliet pushed herself up and stood next to Lu. "Darn Skippy. I can take care of myself and so can my sister. Right, Phee?"

I stood up and handed my wine glass to Clint. "I most certainly can. To make up for your caveman ways, you can pour me another glass of wine."

Clint held up his hand in defeat. "Mercy! Mercy! I give up. I won't be a macho jerk ever again. I'd better start sleeping with one eye open. I'm scared you three will take me out. I'm only a macho ass because I don't want anything to happen to Phee. I'm scared I'd go into the poorhouse trying to feed that ox of a cat of hers."

I slid next to him and put my arm around his waist. "I forgive you this time since you begged for mercy. I'm nothing if not benevolent. Don't let it happen again, mister, or you'll be sleeping in the dog bed with Watson! By the way, my cat is not an ox. He's just big-boned." I leaned in closer and whispered in his ear, "Did you really plan on sleeping tonight?"

CHAPTER THIRTY

I slept in the next morning since it was my day off. I was scheduled to work on Saturday. I promised Mom last week that I would come by and pick up a box of old clothes to donate to the church rummage sale. I cruised slowly down the road singing an Aerosmith tune at the top of my lungs. As I rounded the curve a half mile before my parent's home, I spotted a familiar figure in blue jogging pants with an Irish Setter beside him. Dad and Hamlet moseyed down the road at a leisurely pace, a puff of smoke occasionally drifting past my father's head.

I pulled up next to him and slowed to a crawl. "So, Dad, does Mom know you're still smoking cigars?"

"Nope and tattling on your dad insures you get nothing but coal in your stocking for the next three Christmases." He let a circle of smoke that drifted away on the warm summer breeze.

"Hop in, and I'll give you and Hamlet a ride back to the homestead. No cigars in Velma though. I just washed and vacuumed her. She's all fresh and shiny." I pulled to the side of the road and stopped. Dad opened the back door of the van. Hamlet hopped in and let out a small woof of happiness as he settled onto the rear seat. Dad climbed in the passenger side and I eased back onto the road.

"So what's my favorite daughter up to today?" Dad asked.

"You know Juliet and I talk. You tell her she's your favorite, too," I laughed. "The gig is up."

"You're all my favorites," Dad said with an innocent air. "Your mom's driving me crazy with all this rabbit food she keeps stuffing into me. I'm so hungry Hamlet is starting to look like a leg of lamb."

"So you're pretending to jog, then go out and smoke? Mom will murder you if she catches you."

"I have one cigar a day. Life is full of little pleasures. All I want out of life is a great dinner cooked by your beautiful mother, an expensive brandy and cigar with my favorite novel, and happy children. Is that asking too much in my old age?"

"You're not old, Dad. And no, it's not, but you know Mom is only thinking of your health when she feeds you carrots instead of carrot cake," I said.

"I know. I love your mother, so I hide my cigars and brandy because it makes her worry. Marriage is full of compromises and white lies," Dad advised.

"Dad! That's horrible. You're telling me to lie? Nice," I drawled.

"Is it really lying if you don't say something to spare the other person's feelings? I don't tell your mom I smoke cigars and she's happy. She doesn't tell me how much she spent on those horrible curtains in the den and I'm happy."

"I'm shocked and appalled," I laughed. "You should write a book called *Dad's Words of Wisdom for Wedded Bliss*."

"Speaking of relationships, how are you and Clint?"

"We're fine. He got back Monday from a five day workshop, and I got to meet his new partner, Lucinda," I said. "Dad, did you ever meet Clint's parents before they died?"

"I didn't know his mom had died. When did it happen? You should have told us. We would have come to the service," Dad said. "I never cared for the woman, but I would have gone out of respect for Clint."

"What?" I said confused. "Wait a second. I thought Clint's parents died when he was a kid."

"Honey, you definitely need to talk to Clint about this one. All I know is gossip and innuendo. I don't know the full story, so I don't want to tell you something that's not true. I remember promising his aunt not to mention his dad's death. Everything was hushed up to protect him. Clint's mom dumped him on the aunt's doorstep and took off. As far as I know, she hasn't been back to see him since."

"He never talks about his parents. I just assumed they were both dead. I didn't want to bring up a painful subject for him." I pulled into the driveway and turned off the van. I sat there shocked by my dad's revelation.

"From all the gossip at the time, it's not a pretty story. But again, I'm not the person to tell you about it. I don't even think Rick knows the whole story," Dad said.

"I'm dumbfounded that I don't know anything about Clint's family. How could I know him for this many years and be so clueless?" My hands still gripped the steering wheel, and I stared out the front windshield. I realized I was walking through life and love half-blind.

"Honey, Clint's always been closed off and quiet. Just because you're dating, doesn't mean he'll magically change. You date a man for who he is, not the man you think he should be. Can I give you some advice?"

"Please, do. I need some because I don't know how I could be so clueless."

"You're twenty-eight years old but acting like a teenager in this relationship with Clint. I still get that same punched-in-the-gut feeling I did the first time I met your mom, so I understand. We Jeffersons love deeply. It's our curse and our blessing. When it comes to Clint, you need to take off the rose-colored glasses and see if you love the man that Clint actually is, rather than the fantasy you've created in your mind."

"I'm scared to, Dad. He's all I've ever wanted." I teared up.

"I think you'll still love him. I consider myself a pretty good judge of character, and Clint's a good man. He has some demons from his past though, and you need to know what they are."

I leaned over and laid my head on his shoulder. "Thanks, Daddy. I'll talk to him."

"You're welcome, sweetheart. Do me a favor and don't tell your mom I spilled the beans about Clint, okay? She and I made a pact long ago to not interfere in our adult children's lives."

"Does this fall under the chapter called Dad's Marital Musings for a Magnificent Marriage?" I said with a raised eyebrow.

"Definitely. She might take away meat altogether and make me eat tofu if I make her too angry," Dad had the look of a stray cat cornered in a cage as he thought about tofu.

"My lips are sealed. Let's get in there before she suspects we're in collusion. I don't want her to stop making me brownies because she thinks I aided and abetted your secret smoking."

Dad, Hamlet and I went into the house. We found Mom with her head buried in a closet in my old room. She pulled out a large cardboard box and emerged triumphant. Her hair was in disarray and her cheek bore a smudge of dirt. The grin that split her face was pure mischievous elf. My mom might be nearing sixty, but she was a teenager in spirit. "I finally got it, darn it!"

I rushed forward and took the heavy box from her arms. "I've got it, Mom. Is this the only box?"

"For now. I have a few coats I'll bring out to the van. Your father can carry the small box I put together of old books and knickknacks for the sale."

We carried out the donations and loaded them into the back of Velma. Mom promised me breakfast in exchange for hauling the boxes, but after the blueberry faux cakes on Sunday, I was a little gun shy. I felt a little thrill of pleasure as Mom pulled a quiche from the oven. "Mmm...it smells great," I lifted my nose in the air and inhaled. My mom's cooking really was a little slice of happiness. No wonder my dad was depressed with the change in diet.

"It is made with free-range eggs, low-fat cheddar cheese and turkey bacon. I think you'll be surprised how close it tastes to the higher fat version. I even made real coffee for you," Mom said as she set the quiche on a trivet in the middle of the table. "How did dinner with the Senator go?"

"It was actually a very pleasant evening after we stopped talking about his daughter's murder. He's an interesting person with concrete ideas on how he wants to initiate change. I'm impressed. I liked his aide, Anthony, too. He's a hoot and a phenomenal chef."

"Sheila said Jaime is pulling his hair out over this murder," Mom said as she handed me silverware and plates to set the table.

"The Senator thinks it was Elody's boyfriend who killed her. I have to admit that he is the most obvious suspect," I said.

"I think I saw that Jay Burns character at the lake this morning when I was jogging," Dad said as he came into the kitchen. "Darker hair pulled back into a ponytail?"

"Yes. Good-looking if you like the Rico Suave look. He has a bunch of tattoos."

"Then it was definitely him. He must not be too heartbroken over Elody's death. I saw him in a hot lip lock with an attractive brunette. Maybe Jaime should pull him in for further questioning. I bet he'd like to know about Jay's new love interest," Dad said.

"Was this brunette short with a slim build?" I asked.

"I think so. I jogged past them with Hamlet and only got a brief look. They jumped apart when I rounded the curve of the path and tried to act like they were just talking, but I know what I saw."

"You're jogging and new healthy lifestyle might have cracked the case wide open, Dad. Way to go!" I winked at him and we shared a secret smile.

CHAPTER THIRTY ONE

I spent the morning with my parents and ended up with another box of donations. Mom asked me if I would pick up a box from Mrs. Willoughby before dropping everything at the church. Since Mrs. Willoughby was ancient and shouldn't be driving, I promised I would. I figured it was my civic duty to protect the town from her bad driving.

I steered Velma towards Lakeshore Drive and Mrs. Willoughby's lakeside cottage. I passed a cluster of rental cabins and spotted Jay putting a canvas into the back of an SUV and head back inside. I pulled in to see if I could get more information. I hopped out of Velma and walked nonchalantly to the back of his vehicle and glanced in the open rear. I was shocked to see one of Elody's paintings from Stone Street Gallery. Maybe Kevin was wrong and Jay had purchased them, not the Senator.

"Phee, what are you doing here?" Jay appeared by my side. He reached up and shut the back of the SUV and leaned against the rear bumper. Although his expression was friendly, his hands coiled into tight fists and he looked poised to fight. "Not that I'd ever turn away the company of a pretty girl."

"You're good for my ego," I twittered in my best attempt at flirting. "I was on my way to pick up some things from a family friend when I spotted you. Can I be honest with you? I don't know anything at all about art and everyone keeps raving about yours. Could you do me an itsy-bitsy favor and show me some of your paintings?" I looked at him from under my eyelashes. Juliet might think she ruled when it came to dancing with the enemy, but I claimed my crown with this performance.

Jay relaxed and pushed off the bumper. "Sure. I've got a piece I'm finishing up right now. Come on inside."

I hesitated for a moment over my foolish impulse. Did I really want to be alone with a possible killer? "Okay. Let me call and let Mrs. Willoughby know I'll be a few minutes late."

"Come inside when you're done then." He walked into the cabin.

I hit the speed dial for Juliet. "Juls, no time to talk. I'm at Jay's cabin at 325 Lakeshore Drive. He's going to show me his paintings. If I don't call you back in twenty minutes, send help."

"What? Are you crazy? Hold on!" Juliet sputtered, but I hung up before she could say anything else. I gripped my keys in my hand as a makeshift weapon and went inside.

"Over here," Jay said and motioned me to come next to him. He had a large painting on an easel. It looked finished to me, but he had a palette and brushes on a stand next to it. I thought I spotted some silver-handled paintbrushes in a clear jar on the windowsill, but couldn't tell for sure. "This piece is dedicated to Elody and our love."

I examined the painting. It was a painting of a man and a woman entwined and incorporated into the boughs of an oak tree. I peered closely and saw the same unique brush strokes of Elody's other paintings. "This is amazing! You can definitely add me to your fan club," I gushed.

"Thank you. I need to add a little more detail and I want to make the colors darker. I started this before Elody died. Back then, the world seemed bright and shiny. With her gone, it is gray and dreary. I want this to portray the transition from light to dark."

"That's so sweet. Elody was lucky to have you in her life. Thank you for showing this painting to me. Do you have any others here?" I looked around the room but didn't see any.

"Not right now. I have another one I'm finishing, but I'm not ready to show it to anyone. You'll have to wait until it's displayed at Stone Street Gallery in a few weeks." Jay slid closer to me. "I'm glad you've joined my fan club. I'm flattered a beautiful woman likes my work."

"Are those paintbrushes on the windowsill antiques?" I asked.

"I'm not sure. A friend gave them to me as a gift this week. I think she was trying to cheer me up after everything that's happened." He moved closer and looked as if he planned to put his arm around me.

I sidestepped him and looked at the watch on my wrist. "You are so talented. Thank you again for showing me your work. I'd better hurry if I'm going to make it to my friend's house. I'll be sure to come to the show."

I fled to my van and sped off. Jay probably thought I was crazy, but his ability to turn his grief over Elody off and on so quickly disturbed me. I'd felt like a rabbit charmed by a cobra. Unlike the doomed rabbit, I broke free. I picked up my cell phone and called Juliet. "I'm safe."

"Thank the goddess. If anything happened to you, I'd have to go into witness protection to save my hide from Clint's wrath. Don't ever pull a stunt like that again," Juliet commanded.

"I saw an opportunity and took it. I was smart enough to call you and let you know where I was. He isn't dumb enough to hurt me when he knows someone expected me. Hello? Didn't just crawl out from under a rock yesterday."

"Hmm…that's a matter of opinion. Did you find anything?" Juliet asked.

"As a matter of fact, I did. Jay showed me one of his paintings. If he hadn't told me it was his, I would have sworn Elody painted it. He also had one of her paintings from the gallery in the back of his car. Didn't Kevin say the Senator bought them?"

"Yes, he did. That's weird. Let me call Kevin and see if maybe we misunderstood. I'll call you right back." Juliet disconnected.

I parked in Mrs. Willoughby's driveway and got out. She must have heard me pull in because she opened her front door and thumped her way out leaning heavily on her cane. "Ophelia, come inside. I've got that box of donations but come have a glass of lemonade with me before you go."

I groaned. Mrs. Willoughby was sweet, but she was deaf as a fencepost and rambled on for ages about the garden club. Now I knew why Mom conned me into this errand. "I'd love to, Mrs. Willoughby. I can't stay long though." I pasted on a bright smile and followed her into the kitchen.

Twenty minutes later I escaped from azalea hell and carried a box of clothes to Velma. I checked my phone and saw three missed calls from Juliet followed by a text message demanding I call her ASAP.

"It's about time!" Juliet answered. "I've got news and you're not going to believe it."

"What? Don't keep me in suspense."

"Someone broke into the gallery last night and stole everything including Elody Campbell's paintings."

"Holy frijoles! I need to see the sheriff and tell him I saw Jay put one of the stolen paintings in his car. I'm leaving the lake now. I'll be back to town in fifteen minutes. Meet me for lunch after I talk to the sheriff?"

"Sure. I'll snag us a table at Odd Couple's and wait for you," Juliet agreed and hung up.

Fifteen minutes later, I charged into the sheriff's office. Tina was on the phone but told whoever was on the other end that she would call them back in a minute. "Another body?"

"No, but I know where some stolen paintings are. Is the sheriff in his office?"

"He's in a meeting at the Mayor's office. Deputy Gifford is here."

"She'll do. Can you let her know I need to speak with her?"

Tina buzzed back and told Lu she was wanted up front. A moment later, Lu appeared around the corner. "Hey, girl. What's up?"

"I just left Jay Burns' cabin a little while ago. I spotted one of Elody Campbell's paintings from the gallery in the back of his SUV. I think he broke in and stole it last night!" I said.

Lu arched an eyebrow. "Are you sure?"

"Definitely. Juliet and I just looked at them yesterday at the gallery. I'm positive it was one of Elody's paintings. He may have more, but I only caught a glimpse. You need to head over there and arrest him."

"Whoa. Cool your engines there, Nancy Drew." Lu put both hands up to stop me. "I'll head over there, but I can't arrest him until I have proof he actually has the paintings."

"I told you that I'm positive it was Elody's painting from the gallery. What more do you need?" I couldn't believe she was wasting time and not going after Jay.

"Maybe things happen differently in Miller's Cove, but in America, you can't just slap cuffs on someone because you *think* he committed a crime. There's this little thing we cops like to call evidence. Let me cruise over to the lake and talk to him. Thanks for stopping by and giving us the information." Lu turned away in dismissal and walked back towards her office.

I blinked my eyes and stared after her. "Phee, I think you just got dissed," Tina said, chomping her gum.

"I can't believe she blew me off like that. How does she expect to catch any criminals with an attitude like that? And here I thought she and I were going to be friends." I glared down the empty hallway.

"The sheriff was kind of a jerk to her this morning at the gallery. Maybe she took her frustration out on you. I think she's actually a darn good cop," Tina offered.

"I hope you're right." I opened the door and stomped out into the muggy heat of the afternoon. In the distance, I heard the rumble of thunder and saw thunderclouds off to the west. "Great. At least the weather matches my mood."

CHAPTER THIRTY TWO

I walked down the sidewalk to Odd Couple's Diner grumbling under my breath about rude people. Several people I passed gave me a wide berth. The wind caught the door as I opened it and jerked it out of my hand. The storm loomed closer and another crack of thunder sounded. Seth hurried forward and grabbed the door to muscle it shut.

"Sorry, Seth. The wind is picking up. I think we're in for a major storm from the looks of the sky," I said.

"I think you're right," Seth peered out the front windows. "Juliet's in the back booth. Want me to bring you a root beer?"

"Ah, you know me all too well," I saw Juliet hunkered down with her nose buried in the latest Laurie R. King mystery. I plucked the book out of her hands and sat across from her. "What's up, chicken butt?"

"I was reading that!" Juliet pulled the book from my grasp and closed it. "You know for a person who is supposed to want people to read, you sure are a buzz kill."

"I'm crabby, and I want to share my gloom and doom," I said. "I told Lu what I saw, and she blew me off."

"Really? So she's not going to investigate?"

"She said she would cruise by and talk to him. She couldn't arrest him based on my say-so," I slumped down in my seat and stabbed a straw into the root beer Seth set in front of me. "This is why people get away with murder."

"Settle down there, cowgirl. Lu said she would check it out, so she will. She's right. You can't haul somebody to jail without any evidence," Juliet said. "If she can see the paintings in the back of the car, then she has probable cause for a search warrant. Right now, all she can do is go question Jay."

"When did you get so smart?" I sucked the last of the root beer up the straw with a loud slurp.

Juliet cringed and pulled the empty glass away from me. "You might want to slow down on the root beer. I wouldn't want you to get sugar drunk this early in the day. For your information, I'm not kidding about going into police work. It's fascinating."

"You would do a better job than Lu," I said grumpily.

"Give her a chance. According to the grapevine, Sheriff Dawes gave her hell in front of everybody this morning. Lu made an offhand comment that most art galleries in New York had high tech security systems and not having one was asking for trouble. The sheriff came unglued and told her that Miller's Cove didn't need big city ideas and big city law enforcement sticking their noses in where they don't belong. I feel sorry for her."

"No wonder she snapped at me. The sheriff's feeling the pressure to solve this case or the state police are going to step in. Even so, he shouldn't have yelled at Lu. She's probably already regretting her move," I said. The last of my anger drifted away and left me feeling like a heel. "I'll invite her to hang out with me this weekend and show her the hidden treasures of Miller's Cove. It'll cheer her up."

"Good idea. While you were chitchatting with Mrs. Willoughby having a grand old time, I made a few phone calls. Turns out that Tessa Brewer is in debt up to her eyeballs."

"How did you find that out?" I asked. Seth walked up and asked for our order. "I'll have a Hammy David Junior with a side of fries and another root beer, please."

"Same here, but hold the root beer. I'll take a refill on my water." Juliet waited until Seth walked away then continued, "I called in a favor with a girl I went to college with. She is a reporter at one of the papers where Tessa does a lot of freelance work. I asked Kami what she knew about her. It might all be hearsay, but Kami said Tessa invested in some real estate deal a year ago and lost a boatload of money. She's been hustling stories to every newspaper in the tri-state area trying to recoup some of her cash."

"Maybe she's trying to con Jay out of some money. Dad spotted Tessa and Jay in a love clinch down at the lake this morning. There's something fishy going down with those two, and I'm not talking about the trout swimming in the water."

"They are in cahoots on something, but we still don't have concrete proof that either one of them killed Elody," Juliet said.

"We know Tessa "discovered" Jay even though they've known each other for years. Elody fought with Jay over something and left him." I ticked off the facts on my fingers. "Elody and Jay's painting styles are so similar they are almost indistinguishable. Tessa carries a gun. Elody was shot. Jay stole Elody's paintings from the gallery. I don't know how much more evidence we need. Do I need to paint a picture for the sheriff to get him to arrest one or both of them?"

"You're preaching to the choir, sis. It's all circumstantial evidence. We should lay the case out for Clint this evening and see what he thinks," Juliet suggested.

"Okay. Let me call him." I rummaged in my bag and pulled out my phone. Clint answered after a few rings. "Hi, sweetheart. Juliet and I wanted to talk to you about the case tonight."

He heaved a sigh of frustration. "Phee, I really wish you'd leave this case alone. I'm up to my eyeballs with evidence, paperwork and frightened townspeople. Can this wait until tomorrow?"

"I'm sorry I bothered you," I said frostily. "I'll call you tomorrow." I hung up before he had a chance to respond.

"Trouble in paradise?" Juliet asked. She shook salt onto her fries and handed me the shaker.

"I don't know, but we're on our own for now. What do you know about Clint's parents?"

"They're dead, aren't they? They died when Clint was a kid. That's why he moved here. Why?" Juliet stuffed a fry into her mouth.

I salted my fries and set the shaker down. I looked at Juliet across the table and said, "That's just it. His dad is dead, but his mom is still alive. Why didn't I know that? I'm his girlfriend. I've known him over half my life, and I've only scratched the surface of his life. What else don't I know about the man sleeping in my bed?"

"Whoa. That's heavy stuff. Did you talk to Rick?"

"No. I haven't had a chance. He's got the big project at work, so I didn't want to bother him. Dad spilled the beans this morning. He said he only knew gossip and told me to talk to Clint. I don't even know how to approach him with it. What do I say? 'Hey Clint, I heard your mom's still alive when everyone thought she was dead. What's up with that?' I'm floundering here. I guess your instincts were right about him. He's not invested in me or our relationship or he would have told me," I stared glumly at my sandwich.

"I wish I had some advice to give you. For the first time in my life, I'm truly speechless," Juliet admitted. She swirled another French fry on her plate and bit it.

"Me, too," I ripped my sandwich in two then dropped it onto my plate. "I'm speechless and clueless."

CHAPTER THIRTY THREE

Juliet and I ate our lunch in silence, each of us lost in our own thoughts. I thought of a hundred scenarios on how I could approach Clint about his lack of communication. In each one, I envisioned a bad ending. Should I keep my mouth shut and not rock the boat? We loved spending time with each other, but everything stayed on the surface. No talks late into the night about our dreams and ideas. We never discussed our future.

"I'm over myself," I leaned back when I ate my last bite of sandwich. "If I don't get up and do something, I'm going to sit here feeling sorry for myself all day. I didn't act like a sad sack before Clint, and I'm certainly not going to be one now. Let's go find something to do."

"I have an evening yoga class to teach to the seniors, but I'm free until then. Let's go visit Willow. She wanted to do a full reading for me. I think you should let her do one for you, too. You don't have to believe, but it will be fun either way. I'll call her and see if we can come by now."

"Why not? Maybe the spirits can tell me what to do because I don't have a clue," I said.

We paid our bill, and I followed Juliet to her apartment to drop off her convertible. She hopped in Velma and we chugged back to the lake to find Willow. Juliet directed me towards a tiny cabin nestled against a large stand of trees. Willow sat outside cross-legged with her head thrown back and her eyes closed. Juliet and I strolled across the grass and stood waiting for her to acknowledge us. A few minutes later, she slowly opened her eyes and straightened her legs. "The spirits are very active today. The storm brings them energy and opens the portal between this world and the next. I have a lot to tell you both."

We followed her into the tiny cabin. It was one room with a loft sleeping area above us. There was a small wooden table in the center of the room, and she invited us to have a seat. In the middle of the table was a wooden bowl filled with a variety of large stones and crystals. I shot Juliet a skeptical look, but she ignored me.

"Phee needs some guidance…" Juliet started but Willow held up her hand to silence her.

"Don't tell me. Let me connect with the spirits and have them guide us," Willow said. "Phee, please choose four stones from the bowl. Don't think about it. Pick ones that call to you."

I rolled my eyes but decided to play along. I pulled the wooden bowl towards me and picked four stones. "Now what?" I asked.

"I want you to close your eyes and think about whatever you need guidance on and transfer those thoughts into the stones. Keep tight hold of the stones as you meditate on your issues," Willow instructed. "Juliet, while she's doing that, choose your four stones."

I closed my eyes and did as she instructed. I thought about Clint and his emotional reticence, Elody's murder and how to catch the killer, and finally, I thought about myself and how I wished I had more confidence. I opened my eyes and saw that while I'd contemplated my problems, Willow had placed four candles on the table and lit them.

The scent of patchouli, sage, lemon and something else filled the air. She moved around the room chanting quietly under her breath. She had added bells to her dreadlocks. They tinkled quietly as she moved.

"I really don't believe in this woo woo stuff," I said apologetically. "I don't know how any of this is going to help me."

"The spirits understand your reluctance to believe, but they are gentle beings and laugh at your willingness to believe in the fantasies you find in the pages of your books but not what surrounds you every day," Willow said in a sing-song voice. She stopped flitting about the table and sat down. "Please hand me your stones, Phee."

I reached across the table and dropped the four stones into her outstretched hand. She placed them one by one next to the four candles. "I'm placing these stones in the four corners represented by the four candles. Each represents earth, fire, water and air. I need you to stay silent while I commune with the spirits."

Willow closed her eyes and rocked back and forth, her lips moving silently. I leaned back in my chair and waited to see what kind of baloney she'd pull out of her dreads. Juliet sat wide-eyed and completely entranced by Willow's act. When we were done, I'd need to have a come back to reality chat with her.

Willow opened her eyes and stared at me. Startled, I felt trapped and drawn to her. I thought for a moment her eyes glinted gold before shifting back to their normal brown. It must be a trick of light from the candles.

"Your first stone is the bloodstone." Willow picked up the greenish-colored stone with flecks of rusty brown. "It brings your courage and purpose in difficult situations. You don't know how to confront a loved one and are fearful of what you will discover. Use your inner strength and know that despite your fear, in the end, all will be revealed."

"Phee, I think she's talking about your problem with Clint," Juliet whispered.

"Silence!" Willow commanded. "Do not interfere with the message." She reached out and picked up another stone. This one was also green. "This is aventurine. It is the stone of opportunity. It will help you release attachments and move forward in your life. The earth spirit tells me you cling to old ideas and beliefs, but you need to release these attachments and embrace new ideas. Change isn't always bad. It can breathe new energy into a tired life or relationship."

I thought about my love of old things. I did have a tendency to cling to the past. Look at my relationship with Clint. I hadn't dated because I was so attached to my teenage crush on him. Would I have become a dried-up spinster if he hadn't fallen in love with me?

Willow picked up the third stone. It was a deep shade of blue. "This stone is blue apatite. It is used to motivate you and to help you communicate with beings on this realm as well as the next. It aids the throat chakra. You sometimes have difficulty expressing yourself in times of turmoil or stress. The spirits tell me you need to believe in your inner voice and allow it to come forth. They also advise that you need to stop disconnecting yourself from other realms and your own spirit. You are too present in this earthly realm to the exclusion of all others. Open your heart and mind to other possibilities. Allow the spirits to communicate and guide you." She picked up the final stone and held it in her hands. "Ah, the moonstone. Its uses are twofold. It protects you as you travel at night or by water. It also assists with love. It aids new love or reunites lovers who part in anger. The spirits tell me you will embark on a journey that will bring closure to a troubled soul. You will be in danger, so guard yourself well. Carry this stone with you at all times."

Willow smiled at me and patted my hand like a wise, old crone. Despite my disbelief in her spirit guides, I felt a sense of calming warmth flow through me. I thought about what she said. All of it was fairly vague and could apply to any situation if you thought about it. Despite my misgivings, I figured this hadn't been an entire waste of time. I'd calmed down from my earlier upset over Lu and my discord over Clint's secrecy. "Thanks, Willow. This helped me," I said.

"You're welcome." She placed the stones in a deep blue velvet bag. She handed the bag to me. "Keep these on you at all times in the coming days. They will bring you strength and wisdom."

"Uh…sure," I said and tucked them into the front pocket of my capris.

Willow turned to Juliet. "Hand me your stones, please." Juliet dropped her four stones into Willow's palm. Willow gazed at them for a moment before placing them next to the four candles. She went through her earlier routine of humming and closing her eyes to commune with the spirits. If nothing else could be said about Willow, she was a consummate actress. She had this gypsy psychic gig down pat. Juliet sat forward in eager anticipation.

"This first stone is called crazy lace agate. It helps you to make decisions. It guides you to balance your emotional and physical worlds so you can choose wisely. The spirits tell me you don't trust your own emotions let alone the emotions offered to you by others. You need to accept that love may be offered freely and received gratefully. There is no harm in embracing it." Willow picked up the next stone. "The second stone is carnelian. You sometimes connect to the spiritual more than the physical world, perhaps out of fear of reality. While the spirits welcome your company, they advise you to be present in the moment and enjoy the gift that life has brought to you. There is great joy to be found in the physical realm and you should embrace it."

Juliet couldn't stop herself. "I bet they are talking about Wade. I should stop fighting his need to commit."

"I don't advise. I am a conduit for the spirits as they send you their message. You must take the message and apply it as the spirits guide," Willow intoned. She picked up the third stone. "Fluorite. An excellent stone to bring one down to earth. This will help you concentrate and learn as you start a new chapter in your life. The spirits see you taking a path that no one expects. Although it will be difficult, they see success and happiness in your future. The fourth and final stone is rainforest jasper. This will help you to hear what others say without judgment or rejection. It balances the male and female energies within us all. It also allows others into our lives while still protecting us. The spirit guides want you to allow love into your life. You are a warm and caring individual who gives love, but sometimes you have difficulty accepting it from others."

Like she did with me, Willow took the four stones and tied them in a bag. Juliet's was green velvet. She took it eagerly from Willow. "Willow, you are so insightful. This has been a great help," Juliet gushed.

"I'm glad I was able to speak to the spirits," Willow said. She leaned forward and blew out the candles. "I wished Elody would have listened to her spirit guides when they tried to warn her."

"Really? What did they say?" Juliet asked.

"Elody's four stones were all tied to protection. The spirits warned of great danger from someone wearing a false face. Trickery and deceit surrounded her on all sides. I wondered if she had her protective stones on her when she died?" Willow mused.

"I'm not sure," I said. "I didn't see them at the crime scene, but I also didn't look that closely when I found her."

"I placed them in a special bag designed to enhance their protection. The silver sheen of the cloth was meant to amplify their protective qualities." Willow shook her head sadly. "She must not have listened to my warnings. Only the spirits know what happened. I can't channel Elody's messages from them now that she has departed the physical realm."

"Too bad. We could really use their help wrapping up this case," Juliet said. "Thanks for your time, Willow. Free yoga classes for the rest of the summer, okay?"

"Sounds like a deal. The spirits wanted me to tell you both to be very careful. The storm that brews outside will hinder you on your night journey. Use caution and guard each other."

"We will. Thanks again," Juliet said. We stood up and stretched. I glanced at the clock on the wall and realized we'd spent over an hour with her.

Juliet and I walked out and got into Velma. The rain started to fall, and the sky had grown darker. I hoped it wasn't the spirits sending us a message about my coming conversation with Clint. I started the van and steered her towards town.

CHAPTER THIRTY FOUR

I dropped Juliet off at her apartment and headed home. I ran from my van in a vain attempt to avoid the rain. Closing the door behind me, I shook my wet curls and set my bag down on the small side table. Ferdie bounded up to me and meowed his annoyance at my long absence. I squatted down and scratched him under his chin. "I know, big boy. You're starving to death because no one ever feeds you."

Walking into my kitchen, I fixed his bowl of kibbles and added an extra spoonful of his favorite canned food on top. I made myself a peanut butter and strawberry jam sandwich with potato chips. I washed it all down with a glass of chocolate milk. Comfort food was a necessity today. I needed to unwind after everything I learned today. I changed into a pair of pajama shorts with kittens chasing balls of yarn printed on them. I browsed the pile of books on the nightstand next to my bed. Should I read the latest Jo Nesbo or reread my favorite Elizabeth Peters' novel? Such is the life of a book loving librarian. Too many books and too little time. I decided to stick with the evening's comfort theme and chose Elizabeth Peters' *Crocodile on the Sandbank*. I settled under my aquamarine sheets and opened the book. Immersed in the misdeeds of Emerson and Amelia Peabody's frustration with him, I didn't realize my cell phone was ringing. I tried to reach across the bed to grab it from the charger but became tangled in the sheets. I finally freed myself and answered with a brusque hello.

"Hi. Is everything okay?" Clint's deep baritone rumbled through the phone.

"Yes. No. I don't know. I couldn't reach the phone and got trapped by my own sheets. Just another nail in the coffin of a crappy day," I grumbled.

"That's part of the reason I called. I'm sure I was one of those nails. I wanted to apologize for earlier. It seems that's all I do lately. I keep sticking my big ole boats in my mouth. I shouldn't have snapped at you. All of us on the force are on edge and short-tempered, but it wasn't fair of me to take it out on you."

"It's okay. Lu snapped at me, too. I heard about the sheriff dressing her down in front of everyone. Is she okay?"

"She's fine. She fumed for most of the day, and Jaime probably shouldn't accept any cups of coffee from her in the next few days if he wants to stay healthy. Getting chewed out occasionally goes with the job. We've all felt the pressure from the Senator and his staff to wrap this case up, but Jaime's at the receiving end of most of it. He hears not only from the Senator's camp, but also the Mayor and the state police."

"Poor Jaime. I'm glad I'm not in his shoes right now. Did Lu tell you what I discovered?" I asked. "And before you say anything, I was careful and made sure someone knew where I was at all times."

"She did. As a matter of fact, she and I got back from questioning Jay a short time ago. There wasn't anything in the back of his vehicle when we got there, but I felt the hood of his car, and the engine was still hot. He could have dumped those paintings anywhere," Clint said.

"Dang it! I thought you guys would be able to link him to at least the recent art thefts. Not that I'm trying to do your job, but everything points to Jay as the murderer. I don't understand why you guys haven't brought him in as a suspect."

"Honestly, he's too good of a suspect. This guy is a street-wise thug. He might as well have a big neon sign over his head that screams "murderer!" I don't doubt Jay's into something illegal, but his M.O. says he's a hands-on criminal. A thief and a brawler, but not a killer. He had to know he'd be suspect number one in Elody's death. I just can't see him making that kind of mistake. If she had disappeared, he'd definitely be my number one suspect, but something just doesn't smell right to me."

"I guess," I said doubtfully. "Elody had a bruise on her face that everyone says came from him. If he had gang connections, I'm sure he's no stranger to guns. He could have one of his homeys bump off Elody. I'm also curious to see what you guys found out about Tessa Brewer. She's someone with something to hide. I'm wondering if it is her teenage criminal past or something else."

"I can't believe my nerdy librarian girlfriend used homey and bump off in the same sentence. Juliet is a bad influence on you, but I'm somewhat intrigued with your edgy new vocabulary," Clint joked. "I've got a buddy in the city running some leads on Tessa. So far everything comes back that she's a reporter with expensive taste in clothing and cars. Although not smart considering her paycheck, it's not a crime to be in debt. We'll have to wait and see what else he finds," Clint said. "Listen, it's been a helluva day. I need to be in the office at the crack of dawn to work on the robberies and the murder. I'll try to stop by your work and see you in the morning, okay?"

"Sure. Clint, once this murder is wrapped up and things settle down, you and I need to sit down and talk about some things. I want to make sure we are both open and honest with each other," I said hesitantly.

"Okay," Clint drew out the word. "I'm an open book, but if you feel we need to talk, we'll talk. Right now, I'm bushed and need to catch some shut eye. I love you, Phee. I'll talk to you in the morning."

"I love you, too. Bye," I said softly. I set the phone down on the nightstand. I think Clint and I had two very different ideas of what constituted an open book. I couldn't fix or deal with anything else tonight, so I nestled back down under my covers, picked up my book and returned to Egypt and the mysteries of the long dead.

I awoke with a start some time later. I must have drifted off while reading. The windows rattled as another boom of thunder shattered the air. I could see shards of lightning cut through the night sky. I decided I'd better make sure my upstairs windows were closed. I dragged myself out of bed and down the hallway to my stairs. Yawning, I went upstairs and closed the upstairs bathroom window. I opened the door to the spare bedroom. Rain pelted through the open window. The curtains billowed out from the wind. I hurried forward and slammed the window shut. I started to close the curtains when I spotted a light flash from inside a car parked across the street. A faint glow was barely visible through the rain-streaked window. I looked again and saw someone sitting in the car smoking a cigarette. Maybe someone dropped off the teenage girl who lived across the street and hadn't pulled out yet. I closed the curtains and headed downstairs.

Still feeling uneasy, I decided to set the alarm. Rick insisted on installing it after last year. I always forgot to set it, but after Willow's dire warnings of danger and the eeriness brought on by tonight's storm, I was on edge. I punched in the code and the panel beeped and showed armed. I peeked through the front window and saw the car still parked across the street. I was being paranoid. I turned off the lamp I'd left burning in the living room and headed to bed. I had to open the library in the morning and story time was scheduled for ten a.m. I hopped back under the covers and turned off the lamp. A moment later, Ferdie jumped on the bed and settled down at my feet. I fell asleep to the sound of rain pounding on the roof.

CHAPTER THIRTY FIVE

My alarm went off at six a.m. I groaned and reached over blindly to turn it off. Missing the lever on the top, it skittered off the nightstand and on to the floor. It's jangling bells caused it to move across the floor like a clock on crack. I rolled over and reached down to push the off switch. Antiques were great most of the time, but this morning was not one of them. I'd give up one of my precious cups of coffee for a snooze button right now. I swung my feet over the side of the bed and slipped on my hot pink bunny slippers with the white fuzzy tails. I scuffed my way to the front door to grab the newspaper. As I opened the door a shrill wailing emanated from my house. Crud! I'd forgotten to turn off the alarm. I punched in the numbers and the ungodly noise finally stopped. I scurried out to grab the paper before my neighbors realized it was me waking them up at the crack of dawn.

The car was still there, and a man sat in the front seat reading a newspaper. Who the heck was sitting in my neighborhood watching us? Enough was enough. I squared my shoulders and marched across the street. I rapped my knuckles on the window startling him. He put the paper down and rolled down the window.

"Excuse me, but who are you and why are you sitting across the street from my house? If you want to talk to me or take pictures of me or whatever you bottom-feeding reporters do, just do it and get out of here!" A flush of anger burned across my cheeks. The paparazzi were worse than a pack of hyenas after an injured antelope. They had some nerve coming to my home.

"Sorry, Miss Jefferson. I didn't mean to upset you. Mr. Ziegfried assigned me to watch your house and make sure nothing happened. Orders are orders."

Flustered, I said, "Anthony asked you to watch over me? Can you get him on the phone for me, please? I want to see why in the world he wants someone guarding my house."

The man pulled a cell phone from the inside pocket of his coat and punched in a number. A moment later, I could hear a voice answer. He handed the phone to me. "Anthony, it's Phee. What in the world is this guy doing sitting outside of my house?"

"Sorry, Phee. I knew you'd say no if I asked you. Tessa sneaking around your house the other night made me uneasy. The Senator and I talked. We both felt it best if we had someone keep an eye on your place at night. If nothing else, it keeps the paparazzi from venturing into your neighborhood. The good thing is that most of them have moved onto greener pastures and newer stories. Miller's Cove should be free of the press by the weekend," Anthony said.

"I really don't think I need a bodyguard, but it was nice of you to worry about me," I said. "Am I allowed to offer him a cup of coffee? I probably gave him a heart attack when I knocked on the car window. I need to give him some kind of peace offering."

"It's fine. He can head back to the cabin and grab some sleep if you're heading to work. I figure you'll be safe in a building full of ankle biters and their parents."

"Hey, those ankle biters are some of my biggest fans!" I protested.

"As president of your fan club, I'm more than happy to welcome them aboard," Anthony joked. "Seriously though, be careful. Saul will be back tonight to watch the house."

"I don't need a babysitter," I argued.

"Please let me do this for at least another day or two, okay?"

I hesitated and then gave in. "Alright. I feel like I should wear an ear bud and have men in dark suits walk next to me."

"Someday soon, I hope the Senator will be that guy. The White House is in his sights, and I hope to be there with him when he reaches his goal. This business with Elody has set him back emotionally, and he's lost some of his drive. I think once they catch the killer, he'll climb back to the top."

"I'm a believer. I thoroughly enjoyed my evening with him. I'd never had the chance to sit down and discuss things with a politician. Senator Campbell seems to be more than just smoke and mirrors. I hope he can recover from this latest personal tragedy," I said.

"He will. I'll check on you later, Phee. Sorry about the scare," Anthony said and disconnected. I handed the phone back to Saul.

"Can I bring you a cup of coffee to make up for you being stuck with Phee duty?"

"Ma'am, it would make my morning."

"I'll be back in a jiffy. Cream and sugar?"

"Black is fine. A cup of coffee will hit the spot. I still need to drive home, and it's been a long night." He stifled a yawn.

I turned and hurried back into the house. I saw Mrs. Lassiter had peeked through her curtains to watch me. I waved to her, and she pulled her head back quickly. I'm sure she thought it unseemly to be out in the street wearing shorty pajamas with kittens and bunny slippers. I started a pot of coffee and dug around in my cupboards for a to-go cup. When the pot gave a final *berrup* and finished perking, I poured a cup and took it out to Saul. He thanked me and said he would see me later this evening. I headed back inside to get ready for work.

Once I arrived at the library, the hours flew. At story hour, moms who stayed at the lake for the summer brought their toddlers for a welcome reprieve. They sat in the corner gossiping quietly amongst themselves while I taught their toddlers how to go on a bear hunt. On Thursdays, I did two story hours. The afternoon group was smaller, but more active than the morning crowd, so I spent more time wrangling active three-year-olds back to the children's area. At four thirty, I dropped into my office chair exhausted.

"This is why I only want two children," Wade declared. "Watching you run after so many kids made me tired. Two kids, a dog and a big tree in the backyard to build a treehouse. The ultimate nirvana for a guy like me."

"Sounds perfect. Does this nirvana include my sister?" I asked.

"I hope so. I've been testing the waters. So far she hasn't run screaming, but she also shies away from talking about any type of commitment. I'm leaving it alone for now. When the time is right, she'll let me know." Wade shrugged his shoulders. "In the meantime, I'll keep drafting my plans for the ultimate tree fort."

"You're a wise man, Wade. Give Juliet time. She's getting there, but you're the first guy who hasn't bored her or scared her away after three months. I have a feeling she'll realize what a catch you are and reel you in like a two hundred pound catfish," I said.

"I'm a slim and trim one eighty. I've been watching my girlish figure." Wade ran his hands down his sides like he had curves. "Don't hate me. Just appreciate me."

I rolled my eyes and laughed. "I'm going to turn off the computers and start shutting this place down. I'm worn out, and I have a standing date with your girlfriend tonight."

"I'll close up if you want to get going. You look like you need a break after today."

"I'll take you up on that offer. See you tomorrow," I said as I grabbed my purse from my desk drawer.

Fifteen minutes later, I was home with my feet propped up and a glass of iced tea in my hand. Juliet called and asked me to pick Shawna and her up at her apartment. Willow had begged off of joining us due to a headache. I told her I'd pick them up at six, and we'd head to Mimi's for dinner. In the meantime, I decided to write down a list of everything we'd learned about Elody's death and see if I could connect all the dots to prove once and for all who had killed her.

CHAPTER THIRTY SIX

I pulled up in front of the antique store at a few minutes before six. Juliet rented the small apartment above the store. She stuck her head out the window and gave me a quick wave. A moment later, she and Shawna climbed into Velma, and we were off to Mimi's for dinner.

Since we arrived early, the dining room wasn't crowded. Tessa sat at a small table in the corner by herself. I asked the hostess to seat us nearby. She must have arrived right before us because she was still looking at the menu. I planned to keep my eyes on her.

"How are things going, Shawna?" I asked. I noticed Shawna made an effort to appear fashionable for our night out. She looked nice with her hair pulled up in a high ponytail and a bit of makeup on her cheeks and eyes.

"I'm okay. Packing up my stuff to head back to the university tomorrow. With Elody's case going nowhere, there's no reason for me to stay. I've got more research to do and need access to the university library," Shawna said. "Thanks for inviting me along. I needed a break from the crickets and critters down at the lake. Communing with nature outside of a lab isn't really my thing."

"In honor of our newly-formed friendship, I made you something," Juliet announced. She reached into her bag and pulled out a hot pink mask.

I groaned and protested, "Don't do it, Shawna. Step away from my sister and her crazy ideas!"

Shawna looked puzzled, but she took the mask from Juliet. "What in the world is this?"

"My sister being a weirdo," I said.

"I'm not a weirdo!" Juliet protested. "I'm inducting Shawna into our crime-fighting team. Every team member needs an official mask." She proceeded to tell Shawna about my attempt to fight book crime last year and my bedazzled ski mask. By the time she was done telling the tale, we were all laughing hysterically. My sister did have a gift for comedy.

"I proudly accept my mask and will wear it whenever I fight crime," Shawna declared. She looked at it. "What's with the 'S'?"

"It stands for Super Scientist," Juliet said. "Mine has a 'Y' for yogi and Phee's has an 'L' for librarian."

"Glad I have an 'S' and not an 'L'," Shawna said. She held up her fingers in the shape of an 'L' to her forehead. "We all know what this means."

"Ha ha. I didn't at the time. I guess I'm not hip to middle school lingo," I said.

We ordered our dinner and spent the evening chatting about everything but Elody's murder. Shawna grew more animated throughout the evening, and I was glad we'd invited her to join us. We finished dinner, and I excused myself to go to the ladies room before we headed back to my house to watch a movie. As I made my way back to the table, I passed Tessa. I overheard her whispering angrily to someone on her cell phone. I squatted down to fix the shoelaces of my Keds and leaned in to listen.

"Jay, you're being paranoid, but I suppose you're right. We'll need to get ahold of that last painting if we're going to pull this off," Tessa whispered. "I'll pick you up in a half hour. Be ready." She snapped the phone shut and noticed I was nearby. Her venomous glare made me finish fumbling with my shoe and scurry back to our table.

"I just overheard Tessa talking to Jay on her phone. They're planning another theft. We need to follow her," I said in a low voice. "Be casual and act like we're heading off to my house to watch movies."

We stood up and made our way towards the exit. "I can't wait to watch an old black and white movie," Juliet said in a loud voice. "I love Cary Grant. I want to butter him like a biscuit and eat him with a side of honey."

"Cool it with the bad acting, Juls. I said casual, not crazy," I hissed. Shawna snorted and clapped her hand over her mouth to keep from laughing.

We climbed into Velma and waited for Tessa to leave. A few minutes later, she exited the restaurant and climbed in to a dark Mercedes. Gunning the engine, she squealed out of the parking lot and shot down the street. I started Velma and followed behind her. Velma wasn't a sports van, so we chugged slowly along keeping several blocks behind Tessa. I wasn't worried. I knew where she was going.

"I wonder what painting they plan to steal?" Juliet mused. "I thought every single one of Elody's paintings had already been snatched."

"Not all of them. I know exactly where she's going," I said with a grim smile. "The Senator has one painting of

Elody's left hanging in his den. I bet that's what they plan to steal."

"They'd have to be crazy to try to break into the Senator's cabin," Shawna said.

"I'm sure they've got some kind of scheme cooked up. Jay and Tessa might clean up well, but their criminal ways always come out," I said.

I pulled over to the side of the road and put Velma in park. Turning towards Shawna and Juliet, I said, "It's decision time. Do we go to Jay's cabin or do we head to the Senator's?"

"I vote the Senator's place," Juliet said. "It's the only place left with a painting. They've stolen the ones from Shawna's cabin and the ones from the gallery. We've got one chance to catch them in the act. I say onward, Jeeves!"

"Shouldn't we call the police and let them handle this?" Shawna piped up from the back seat. "What are three chicks in a van going to do to stop them? Jay's kind of scary, too."

"What are we going to tell the police? We think they're going to break into the Senator's and steal a painting of an unknown artist? Who's going to believe us? What if we're wrong?" I asked. "You can stay in the van and keep watch if you'd like, but I'm tired of sitting on the sidelines and living through my books. I say on to the Senator's."

"You're right. Let's do it. Elody was my only friend and I owe her. To the Senator's!" Shawna cheered and pumped her fist in the air.

I maneuvered Velma back onto the road and towards the lake. Fifteen minutes later, I slowed to a crawl and killed Velma's headlights as I eased to a stop about a hundred yards from the Senator's cabin. Several lights were on and I could see someone on the back porch. We sat in silence and watched.

We didn't have to wait long before Jay's dark SUV zipped past us and pulled in front of the cabin. Jay got out and knocked on the front door. Senator Campbell answered and invited Jay inside. The door closed behind them.

"It doesn't seem like Jay's planning to steal anything," Juliet whispered. "Maybe he plans on conking the Senator on the head and making off with the painting. Of course, that wouldn't be too smart."

"Wait," I hissed back. I could see the Senator and Jay walk out onto the back deck. The stillness of the night and the lake carried their voices up the hill to where we sat. Although I couldn't make out all the words, Jay seemed to be asking for the Senator's help in setting up some kind of fund in Elody's name. I shook my head. I couldn't be hearing him right.

"Who's that?" Shawna pointed towards the cabin. A dark figure had exited the back seat of Jay's car and slunk towards the cabin. The shadow eased the cabin door open and slipped inside. In the brief flash of light before the door closed quietly behind her, I saw Tessa's face.

"We've got to get down there and warn the Senator!" Juliet exclaimed.

"You're right. Hand me my mask," I demanded. Juliet reached into her bag and pulled out my hot pink mask. I slipped it on over my strawberry red curls and stuck my cell phone into my pocket.

"I'm coming with you," Juliet said. She slipped her mask on, too. "Shawna, if we're not back in fifteen minutes, call the police. Tell them someone's trying to rob the Senator, and you thought you heard shots. That'll make sure they hurry and get down here."

"Alright," Shawna said, nerves making her voice shake. "Be careful."

Juliet and I snuck down the hill towards the cabin. We slipped behind trees and once we got near the house, we dropped to our knees and crawled the remaining few feet until we were directly underneath the deck.

"Senator, I understand your reservations about working with me considering my past, but I've turned my life around. I'm an honest person trying to hone my artistic craft through painting and acting. Setting up a grant in Elody's name to fund other young artists would honor her memory. I've got a friend who has set up and managed other memorial grants. She's willing to help us," Jay said, his voice taking on a wheedling tone. He might be suave around women, but around an alpha male like the Senator, he reverted to the mangy cur he was.

"I'm not interested in forming any kind of alliance or partnership with you at all, Jay. Not after what you put my daughter through," Senator Campbell replied.

I touched Juliet on her shoulder. Using hand motions, I indicated I was going to peek in the windows to see where

Tessa was. Juliet nodded her understanding. I eased away from the deck and inched myself along the side of the cabin, pressing my body tightly against the walls to avoid being spotted. Once I made it to the living room window, I stood on my tiptoes to peer through the window. I watched Tessa reach up and slowly take the painting from the wall and head for the front door. I had to stop her. I moved as swift and silent as a jungle panther towards the corner of the cabin. Once there, I peeked around the corner. Tessa eased the door of the cabin open and slipped outside with the painting clutched under her arm. She moved towards the SUV and popped open the back door.

"Stop right there, Tessa," I said in the most authoritative voice I could muster. "Put your hands up and back away from the car."

Tessa set the painting in the back of the car and stepped away from the car. She turned and pointed a gun straight at me. "Take off the stupid mask."

I pulled the mask from my head, and my curls tumbled down around my shoulder. I dropped it to the ground. "Tessa, you don't have to do this."

"What do we have here? A nosy little librarian who doesn't know when to leave things alone. I've had about all I can stand of this backwater town and interfering busybodies," Tessa spat.

"The gig is up, and the police are on their way. You might as well give yourself up. You'll get a slap on the wrist for the art thefts. If you testify against Jay, I'm sure they'll cut a deal. The police are more interested in a murder than the theft of a few cheap paintings," I said in a calm voice.

"You've got this all figured out, don't you, Nosy Parker?" Tessa gave a nasty laugh. "Jay's just a putz with more gambling debts and bad habits than he can afford. The one talent he has is seducing stupid women. That man could charm the crown off Queen Elizabeth herself."

"He didn't kill Elody?"

"Of course not, but he makes a great fall guy, doesn't he? A few articles hinting at abuse. A stray paintbrush left at the scene. Poor, stupid Jay. I'll send him cigarette money while he waits on death row."

"Why did you do all this?" I asked, trying to keep her talking.

"I got stuck covering the club scene with all those trust fund Barbies. I didn't crawl my way out of the peanut fields of Arkansas to bow to the rich and shallow. I happened to see Elody painting one day and realized she actually had talent. Not that she cared or used it. Poor Elody. Can't finish her paintings because her mommy died of cancer," Tessa mocked. "I have a friend who collects art. I showed him a picture I'd snapped of Elody's work and he went crazy. He offered me a finder's fee of ten thousand dollars if I introduced him to the artist."

"You set her up, didn't you?" I said, shocked at the manipulative skills of this woman. I wanted to hear the rest, but I kept my eyes trained on the gun pointed at me. I hoped she didn't have an itchy trigger finger.

"It was like shooting fish in a barrel," Tessa said. "I needed money and those stupid club kids made it so darn easy. I'd run into my childhood buddy, Jay, a few years ago and we'd kept in touch. Fate was looking out for me. He worked in a shop painting murals on motorcycles for wannabe yuppie bikers. I cleaned him up and bought him a new wardrobe. He "bumped" into Elody when she was drunk at one of her nightclub jaunts. Jay kicked in his famous charm. A month later, Elody was caught – hook, line and sinker. Jay convinced her he needed help to get his career started. She didn't give a rat's ass about her art since her mom died. She'd paint the pieces. Jay would add a few odd daubs of paint, then put his name on them. All I had to do was make sure he was "discovered" and the money started rolling in. Elody didn't have any money since Daddy had cut her purse strings, so she didn't complain. I got my cut and everything was great until Jay got stupid and hit Elody. The gig was up. No paintings, no sales, no money. Elody gets a bug up her butt and pulls a disappearing act."

"But I still don't understand why you killed her," I said, stalling for time. Surely Shawna had called the police. I just needed to keep Tessa talking until they got here.

"Elody threatened to expose Jay as a fraud. Do you realize his paintings sell for well over ten thousand dollars apiece? That's a drop in the bucket for someone with Elody's trust fund, but it was a huge bonus for someone living on a measly reporter's salary. I still have a couple of paintings held back as an insurance policy. They'd be worthless if word got out that Jay was a fake. She made the mistake of telling Jay her plan to come clean. She wanted to paint and "honor her inner woman" or some such crap. If you ask me, she missed daddy's money. Selling her paintings would be the only way she could eat if Senator Campbell didn't loosen the purse strings. Elody didn't even realize her relationship with Jay was a scam from start to finish. I've worked too hard to have it all come tumbling down because of some spoiled rich girl. I waited until she was alone in the park and shot her. She never even realized what was coming. She thought I was trying to get her picture for some tabloid. 'Tessa, why can't you leave me alone. Find some other celebrity to stalk.' Waa waa," Tessa imitated Elody's words. "I wish I had her tough life as a poor little rich girl. The only thing my daddy ever taught me was how to drive fast and think even faster. My mama died when I was only three years old. I never had even a half a chance at a good life. Elody had everything handed to her, and she spit on it like a spoiled toddler. She didn't deserve the talent she had. I just wanted one little break in life."

I heard the sound of sirens in the distance. So did Tessa. "Time for you to learn the value of silence. I've already planned the headline. "Boyfriend's Murderous Mayhem at Miller's Cove." Jay killed Elody, then in a fit of rage, he shoots the Senator and an innocent bystander. In a final twist, he turns the gun on himself. The papers will eat it up. I'll be the first reporter on the scene. The scoop will guarantee me a weekly column and a big salary." She leveled the gun at me ready to fire. I closed my eyes and waited for the end.

"I don't think so." There was a loud *thwap* and the sound of something falling. I opened one eye and saw Anthony standing over Tessa's body, a flashlight raised above his head. He must have struck her and knocked her out. I sank to the ground.

"Thank goodness. I saw my life flash before my eyes. It was so boring I almost fell asleep," I joked in relief.

"You're lucky I was reading in my room and heard everything. I guess she figured the Senator was by himself," Anthony said.

"Jay's on the deck with the Senator!" I warned.

Anthony kicked Tessa's gun away from her hand and rolled her over. He felt for a pulse on her neck. "She's out cold, but just in case, grab her gun and make sure she stays put." He reached down to his ankle holster, pulled out a gun, and went into the cabin.

"Holy cow! Phee's got a gun!" Juliet squealed. "I saw and heard everything. She pulled that gun out, and I froze like a deer in the headlights. You could've been killed. Some cop I'd make. First sign of danger and I'm useless."

"It's okay. I would've probably done the same thing. Thank goodness Anthony was here. Otherwise, I'd be waking up tomorrow at the pearly gates instead of in my nice, comfy bed."

The door to the cabin swung open and Anthony pushed Jay out in front of him. Jay stumbled and fell to the ground. Senator Campbell followed behind with a thunderous look on his face. Jay attempted to get up, but the Senator walked forward and punched him. "That's for laying a hand on my daughter, you worthless piece of gutter trash!"

"Whoa! The Senator's B.A.!" Juliet exclaimed.

"You ladies didn't see a thing. He hurt himself when he fell," Senator Campbell instructed.

"Yes, sir," Juliet and I said in unison.

Two patrol cars pulled up. Sheriff Dawes stepped out of one and Clint and Lu jumped out of the other. Anthony walked up to me and slipped the gun gently from my grasp.

He leaned forward and whispered in my ear, "Let me handle this. I'll tell them you and your sister stopped by to pick up a CD of my band I promised you. You stumbled upon Tessa breaking into the cabin and the rest is history. I won't reveal your, uh, interesting attire." He looked at me and smiled.

"Okay," I whispered back. I glanced up and saw Clint cast an inquiring gaze in Anthony's direction. I met his eyes, and he scowled.

"Dang it, Phee! I can't believe you got yourself mixed up in this mess. You could have been hurt," Clint said trying to control his anger.

"I'm sorry. I don't believe we've met," Anthony stepped forward and held out his hand. "I'm Anthony Ziegfried, the Senator's aide. It's my fault Phee got dragged into this mess. I promised her a copy of a music CD we listened to the other evening. She stopped by to pick it up. She and Juliet were innocent bystanders who merely stumbled upon a crime. If not for Phee's quick thinking, Tessa Brewer would have escaped and gotten away with Elody's murder. You should thank your lucky stars you have a brave, beautiful woman like her."

"I, um, I sure am lucky. You're the Senator's lap…aide," Clint stuttered, clearly off kilter with Anthony's smooth explanation. "I'm sorry, Phee. I got a call from some woman saying you and Juliet were in danger and the Senator's house was being robbed. I was terrified I wouldn't get here in time." He pulled me to him and hugged me close. "I'm glad you're okay."

Senator Campbell cleared his throat and said, "I've got to say that Phee was extremely brave. I wish more people got involved rather than looking the other way. Neighbors looking out for neighbors. It's the way it used to be and should be again."

"You're right, Senator," Sheriff Dawes stepped forward. "I taught these two girls everything they know. In fact, I've been thinking Miller's Cove should have a neighborhood watch program. Who better to lead it then Phee and Juliet."

Juliet grinned with excitement at the prospect of sanctioned crime fighting. I groaned as I realized the sheriff had just fueled Juliet's crime-fighting obsession. Pretty soon everyone in town would be wearing pink masks bedazzled with their initial.

CHAPTER THIRTY SEVEN

I dropped Juliet off at her apartment close to midnight. Jay protested his innocence, but Anthony told the sheriff everything Tessa confessed while holding me at gunpoint. Once Jay found out Tessa had set him up to take the fall for Tessa's murder, he sang like a choir boy. Sheriff Dawes even let Juliet slap the cuffs on Jay. After we promised to come down to the station first thing in the morning, the sheriff told us to go home and get some rest. Exhaustion from the late hour and the emotional drain of being held at gunpoint caught up with me. I struggled to keep my eyes open the few miles to my house. I pulled into my driveway. Clint's truck pulled in behind me. I dragged myself up the steps, and he followed me inside.

"Phee, I know you think I'm a jerk, but I just want to keep you safe. That's my job. Not just as a cop, but as your boyfriend," Clint said as we both fell onto the couch exhausted.

"I'm too tired to talk about this right now, but you and I do need to talk. I'm not the same lily-livered girl you fell in love with last year. I've changed. I'm tired of being the nice, predictable girl next door."

"What's wrong with being the girl next door?" Clint asked, concern in his eyes. "I like you just the way you are."

"It's not like I plan to go out and commit bank robberies and dye my hair pink, but sometimes I want to walk on the edge. Live a little dangerously. Stop being scared to stand up for myself. I don't know. I'm saying I want more out of life than going to work then coming home to read a book until I fall asleep," I confessed.

"I can understand that, I guess," Clint said slowly. "The only thing I ask is that you be honest with me about what you're doing. Don't think I didn't see that pink bedazzled mask lying on the ground at the Senator's place. I recognized Juliet's handiwork."

I gave Clint an incredulous look. Despite my exhaustion, I felt a quick bite of anger at his use of the word honest. "I think we both need to be honest with each other, don't you?"

"What are you talking about?" Clint looked puzzled. "I don't hold things back from you."

"Really?" I snapped. I sat up and faced him. "How come we never talk about your past or our relationship? Do you realize that all this time I thought both your parents were dead? You keep everything bottled up and hidden from me. Clearly, you aren't in this relationship for the long haul."

"Wait a minute. I told you when we started seeing each other that I wanted to take it one day at a time. I made no promises. I thought you understood that."

"Well, things change. I need to know that we're going somewhere and I'm not spinning my wheels waiting for you to want something real. I want a family one day. Something concrete and real, not just a fantasy left over from my teenage dreams."

Clint wouldn't meet my eyes. He stared at the wall in front of him, his face a hardened mask of steel. "I love you,

Phee. I love you so much it scares me. I never wanted to care this much about one person, but there's something about you that grabs at my very soul." He slammed his fist down on the arm of the couch. "Damn it! I swore that I would never be stupid enough to fall in love, but that ship's sailed and here we are. You need to realize and accept that I don't ever want a family. I wouldn't be a good husband or a good father. I don't talk about my parents because if you knew the whole story, you'd never look at me the same way again and I couldn't bear it. I'm damaged goods, Phee."

I reached out my hand to grab his, but he pulled away. "I need to go. We're both tired and upset. I need some space and some time to think. I love you, Phee, but you've got to give me some breathing room." He stood up and walked out the front door.

Stunned, I leaned back and rested my head on the couch, tears streaming down my face. What could be so horrible that I wouldn't love him? Had I made a mistake pushing Clint to open up to me? Maybe Clint's past would be the one mystery I couldn't solve.

THE END

ABOUT THE AUTHOR

Amy Lilly grew up in the small town of Cedaredge, Colorado where she spent her free time reading Nancy Drew mysteries and using her Junior Detective Kit to solve mysteries on her family farm. Amy earned a B.A. in English from the University of Iowa and her M.L.S. from SUNY at Buffalo. She spends her free time raising goats, chickens, a herd of well-fed cats and two hyperactive Jack Russell Terriers. She is married with two sons and two beautiful, smart granddaughters.

PHEE JEFFERSON SERIES

DEATH IS LONG OVERDUE
SUMMER READING IS KILLING ME
PERMANENTLY DELETED (WINTER 2015)

STAND ALONE TITLES

THE ROMANCE REPORT (FALL 2015)